Dr. Morelle and Destiny

Ernest Dudley

Table of Contents

Chapter One 5

Chapter Two 10

Chapter Three 16

Chapter Four 22

Chapter Five 28

Chapter Six 34

Chapter Seven 39

Chapter Eight 43

Chapter Nine 50

Chapter Ten 55

Chapter Eleven 61

Chapter Twelve 66

Chapter Thirteen 72

Chapter Fourteen 76

Chapter Fifteen 81

Chapter Sixteen 86

Chapter Seventeen 92

Chapter Eighteen 96

Chapter Nineteen 102

Chapter Twenty 106

Chapter Twenty-One 112

Chapter Twenty-Two 119

Chapter Twenty-Three 124

Chapter Twenty-Four 132

Chapter Twenty-Five   135

Chapter Twenty-Six   141

Chapter Twenty-Seven   146

Chapter One

THE PARTY AT the Post Hotel was in full swing. U.S. Army personnel and their wives, or German girl-friends, the war had been over more than three years, milled around; cigar-smoke and a variety of exotic scents filled the atmosphere, champagne corks popped, there was plenty of back-slapping and laughter. A local dance-band had been brought in to play American jazz with a Teutonic lilt. Plenty were dancing in the big dining-room, decorated with coloured lights. The party was going great.

Outside the Post Hotel the town of Mittenwald, snug beneath the Alps, which had not long ago looked down on a desperate swarm of frightened refugees and fugitives, from Nazi officers and generals to politicians, fleeing from the advancing American troops, looming like white, ghostly towers in the darkness, was blanketed with snow. The narrow street of shops was bright with Christmas decorations, the low roofs glistened white.

Johnny Destiny turned from the window overlooking the street, drained his glass of champagne, and glanced at his watch, pushing back the heavy gold identity-tab he wore low on his wrist. He looked slim and dapper in his Third United States Army sergeant's uniform, his fancy-dress was how he privately regarded it. Taking a drag at his cigarette, he made his way round the crowded floor, eyeing the dancers until he paused to cut in on a big lieutenant who was dancing with a blonde girl.

"Hello, Johnny," she said. She slipped easily into his arms, while the big lieutenant scowled and went off in search of alcoholic consolation. "I was wondering where you were." She spoke English well, with a soft Bavarian accent.

"I been thinking," Johnny said. "I been thinking it's time we took off."

"Whatever you say, Johnny," she said, and smiled into his pale, glinting eyes.

"Get your coat, hon," he said, and patted her wrist on which was the gold watch he had given her for a Christmas present. He watched her, her curves shown off alluringly by the Paris frock she was wearing, slip quickly through the crowd with a stare of mingled admiration and speculation. Her

5

name was Minna Borgmann. She was nearly nineteen. She reappeared with the fur coat which he had also given her over her slim shoulders.

He stubbed out his cigarette and they went out together into the street, where he found the Mercedes coupé which he had parked in the shadows round a corner from the hotel. This was a Christmas present he had given himself. He had stolen it two days before.

Minna got into the car and he slammed the door shut, and got in after her. The Mercedes drove off with a thunderous roar, and soon was speeding out of Mittenwald over the white roads. Johnny drove with one hand, the other arm was round Minna's waist, his hand cupping her breast. Two or three times he let go the steering-wheel to put both his arms round her. She implored him to stop if he wanted to kiss her, she was frightened there would be an accident, the car would skid on the icy road.

He only grinned at her in the glimmer of the dashboard-light. He took the steering-wheel between his knees and steering the car without slackening speed he held her in both arms and kissed her. She was breathless with fright and the intensity of his kisses and then he grasped the wheel again.

"You really love me?" he said, from the side of his mouth.

She pouted at him reprovingly, her red mouth smudged. "Johnny, darling," she said, her eyes brilliant, "don't you know I do?"

There was no smile on his thin face. "I'm not sure," he said. "I wish I could be sure of something."

His mind went back over the rackets he'd been in since the war had ended. There'd been the spell at Hamburg, recovering from the pulverizing it had received from the Allied air forces, where there had been plenty of Germans prepared to do business. He had found it easy to contact the right people, those with diamonds, not the industrial stuff but the real sparklers, and gold and platinum, cameras and liquor, antiques and carpets.

The krauts wanted food and cigarettes and soap in exchange. He'd been able to supply that demand, all right. There'd been a German girl then, too, who'd acted as his go-between and whom he had loaded with silk stockings, jewellery. There'd been a gold watch and a fur coat for her, too. Through various agents he had disposed of the gold and platinum in Brussels and Antwerp, the diamonds on the Antwerp Diamond Bourse, and other stuff through ships sailing in and out of Hamburg for London and other ports.

There was the coffee and cigarettes he'd run into the battered city of Berlin, netting him five thousand dollars a trip; smuggling arms, which were left lying in enormous stocks round about Hamburg, to Mediterranean ports, *en route* to Morocco or the Middle East. He had linked up with a mob in Belgium, mostly deserters from Allied forces, who stole cars and trucks as they were unloaded and ran them down to Spain. There was another racket, smuggling German automobiles across the Channel, and works of art, and suites of furniture.

Then when he had moved south, to Garmisch-Partenkirchen, he had made contact with some ex-SS types and an ex-agent for the *Abwher*, who were pumping drugs into Switzerland, with Paris dope-addicts as their ultimate destination.

Johnny had liked it at Garmisch-Partenkirchen, not so much the wonderful mountains rising on every side, or its swift-flowing River Loisach, with its pretty wooden bridges, which ran through the town on its way to the Danube, but the night-clubs and hotels, the bars and *weinstubes*, where he did business, that he liked. He had never had it so good. Just off a street where the shiny Cadillacs and army trucks shoved the oxen-drawn carts out of the way, he occupied a villa with Minna.

It was here that he and Minna now arrived, to find another party under way. Minna's friends, U.S. Army personnel and Johnny's German stooges were already taking care of the champagne and the food which loaded the tables. Dance-music from the radio filled the villa. After a while, Johnny his expression abstracted, left Minna dancing with a fat American colonel, and went upstairs to the luxurious bedroom, and made a phone call.

The phone call sent him a few minutes later slipping quietly out of the villa and speeding the Mercedes towards Munich, a hundred kilos away. He hadn't stopped to tell Minna he was going to be absent from her party a couple of hours. The party would carry on okay without him.

Driving fast over the icy roads, he found himself in Pariserstrasse, which was one of Munich's less salubrious districts dotted with bars and restaurants. He drew up the Mercedes outside the particular bar he wanted, where the inevitable fruit-machines and skittle-tables were in action, and made his way upstairs. Here in a room overlooking the street, he talked quickly with a grey-faced German, who wore a woollen cap over his round head. What the grey-faced man told him tightened the muscles in Johnny's face, his pale eyes narrowed.

Sixty minutes later he was on the outskirts of Garmisch-Partenkirchen again. He stopped the Mercedes outside his villa, and slipping in the back way, went up to the bedroom. The radio was still going full blast, the party was doing fine.

He packed fast. Money, jewels; plus anything that might be of an incriminating nature.

Then he went downstairs. Hardly anyone seemed to recognize him. No one had noticed apparently that he hadn't been there all the time. The lights had been turned out in the room at the back, and through the half-open door he heard the familiar sounds of semi-drunken love-making. Minna wouldn't be in there, he knew.

She was true to him, in her fashion. Even though, as he knew now, she had been working for the American C.I.C. all the time, she hadn't double-crossed him with any other guy. He was sure of that. He saw her in the front room, with a half-filled glass of champagne in her small hand, listening with a bunch of others to someone spinning smutty stories.

He touched her arm. "Hon, I got a little present I want to show you."

She flashed him her brilliant look, brushed a lock of blonde hair back from her face and followed him upstairs.

"Where have you been darling?" she said. "I missed you —" She broke off as she stood in the bedroom door way and saw the preparations he had made for his getaway.

He had moved swiftly behind the door as she came into the bedroom, wide-eyed. The snout of the Star F .22 L.R. was behind her right ear as she started to turn to him. It was fitted with a silencer and there was hardly any noise at all as the bullet smashed a great hole in her skull. The radio downstairs was drooling out a waltz from the A.F.N. hit parade.

Five minutes later the Mercedes was roaring off along the road for the Swiss frontier town of St. Gallen. Through the misty ravines with the white mountain tops glistening above him against the black velvet sky, Johnny Destiny drove with one hand, but his other arm wasn't around anyone's waist. He was alone, cigarette drooping from the corner of his thin-lipped mouth, his gaze concentrated on the road ahead.

He was going A.W.O.L for a long time.

He lay low in Switzerland a couple of years, moving around from Berne to Lake Lucerne, then Zurich and Geneva. Once in a while he toyed with the idea of returning to the States. He had a dream of setting himself up in Florida, where he'd come from, maybe a gambling setup, or California; or he might try South America. He'd been down to Rio, once, way back. He couldn't be repatriated from South America, and from what he heard there should be something doing there that would suit his dubious talents.

But it was only a pipe-dream. He knew in his heart he would never make it, would never see the States again. Johnny Destiny was quite right about that, too. Though he couldn't anticipate that the reason why he would never see the U.S. again would be quite such a final one.

It was a girl again who gave him the idea about Rome. She was dark-eyed, with a ripe, full mouth and a small, tilted nose like a kitten's, and her name was Carla and she called herself a countess, and he met her in a bar in Geneva. But what interested Johnny most about her was that she could put him in touch with the sort of contacts he wanted to be put in touch with. And Johnny felt like a change of scene, so three years after he had skipped over the Swiss-German border, found him in Rome.

Rome, where Johnny was to dream up a racket which was going to pay off bigger than anything to date. Rome, where he was never to have it so good.

Chapter Two

NOT FOR JOHNNY the Rome of the tourists rubbernecking the museums and art-galleries, the great squares like the Piazza Navona, the Campo del Fiori; the mighty Colosseum, or the pilgrims' shrines such as St. Paul's, San Lorenzo, or San Clemento.

For Johnny it was the Rome which it seemed to him was more vice-conscious, where more rackets flourished than any other city he'd known, New York or Hamburg, Paris or Rio.

To-day, Johnny went through the motions again, he looked in for a pre-lunch cocktail in the Hotel Excelsior on the Via Veneto, not far from the Borghese Gardens, generally referred to as the Snake Pit. He ducked down into the downstairs bar, that sombre dive for people, it seemed to him, who never faced the sun without dark glasses, who couldn't even stand normal indoor lighting.

There was the usual motley mob of Americans drinking Bloody Marys or whiskies, Italians drinking Campari bitters or Cinzano, or Americanos. He took in the local eccentrics and the Hollywood movie-set, plus all the men with beards, who looked too much like artists to be the real McCoy. The usual bunch of Italian counts and countesses, the inevitable cavalcade of gorgeously-dressed girls, either there by assignation, or swinging their hips hopefully and pointing their long Italian shoes coquettishly as they gave the men the speculative once-over.

There was no one who interested Johnny so very much. He had been in Rome several weeks now, he had just about sized it up, with Carla's help, and he was waiting for something to break. He was waiting for the big idea, the bright notion. It was very overdue.

He lit another cigarette and went upstairs to the lobby and the outer bar of the Snake Pit. This was where the fast deals were done, where you waited around looking for that certain someone who might have some tip-off that was worth waiting around for. Johnny knew the men that met his eye. Fat or skinny, mostly old, with too-highly manicured finger-nails, balding heads and anxiety-filled creased faces. They had nothing for him.

Johnny sized up the mob, and strolled over in the summer sunshine to Giorgi's, a block or two away. At Giorgi's he sat down and let Giovanni order his lunch for him while he sipped another Martini, and eyed the others lunching there, most of them were those he had not long left at the Snake Pit.

Then it was time for siesta. The sun was beating down and the shops all closed and the streets deserted and the heat glancing off the shimmering walls, as he took a cab to the apartment he shared with Carla in a large, decaying old palace in the Piazza del Gesu, a barracks of a place, with entrances round the courtyard, and long winding corridors, marble staircases with lofty windows to the innumerable landings. Carla liked to lie in bed all day, and to get up in the evening after siesta-time, which would be followed by making love with Johnny.

He had discovered she was a genuine countess all right, aged twenty-two, and already beginning to run to fat.

That evening Johnny took the cool air with Carla on the sidewalk in front of Doney's, where the crowds milled along slowly, exchanging stares with those sat in the cane-bottomed chairs. Lovers out for a stroll, fathers and mothers with their families out for a stroll, and men in pairs, hunting girls, and girls in pairs, hunting men.

Some of the chichi set still wore their dark glasses, even though night had fallen and the lights winked and glimmered all around the beautiful old city, and the scent of the cool grass crushed by the footsteps of the strolling throngs and multitudinous flowers drifted down from the sprawling Borghese Gardens.

Johnny found himself with Carla inside the Excelsior, everywhere fogged with cigar-smoke and discordant with chatter, so that the place might have been an aviary filled with starlings. The same mob met his pale eyes. The same languorous women, decked out for the evening, were drifting amongst the people who packed round the bar.

Presently after a drink or two each, they moved on to Capriccio's for the eats. They took their time over the anti-pasto, the cacciatore and the sweet, the fruit and the cheese. By the time Johnny and Carla had finished then-brandy, it was pushing midnight. They made their way leisurely along to Bricktop's, just down the hill from the Excelsior. They went through a milk-bar and past a florists to the club, run by Bricktop, a middle-aged, plump American negress with rusty hair scraped up high on her head, and rusty freckles across her broad nose.

Her place was a softly-lit, spacious room, with mirrored walls above comfortable seats, and flowers on the piano. There was no floor-show. Brick sang songs from the 20's and 30's, old Cole Porter numbers, Irving Berlin and Gershwin. She reminded Johnny of New York before the war when he was a new boy in from the Coast, a natty dresser with his grey fedora and light-coloured tie.

It was 3 a.m. when Johnny and Carla went out into the prostitute-haunted streets, the rapacious-eyed women working sometimes singly, sometimes in pairs, and he got a cab and took Carla, back to the Piazza del Gesu apartment. Then he went over to the American Club, just for a nightcap and the walk.

In the bar, which was empty except for a tall blonde with grotesquely false eyelashes and a long amber cigarette-holder just like an international spy, who was arguing in a maudlin way with the bartender, whose weary, chocolate-pouched eyes had seen it all, and whose small ears tight against his dark skull had heard it all, and then some, the big idea came to Johnny.

The notion, it came to him out of nowhere.

Up till then Johnny's ostensible line of business which he had set up in Rome had been import-export, a front which covered a multitude of sins. Peddling nylons, Swiss watches, the old diamond racket, all the usual small-time stuff. Small-time stuff, yes, but together with keeping his ear to the ground and with the tip-off's Carla's contacts had supplied him, he had got enough information into his skull which subconsciously had been the forcing-bed for this new project.

Johnny Destiny came out of the American Club, his brain afire. He hurried past a fat man in dark glasses, chatting to a bunch of early-morning drunks who were too tired and too sad to go home. The canned music from a juke-box in some dive followed Johnny past a crowd of long-haired men and short-haired women and the shabby artistic types, past a slim man whom he knew was on his way from the cabaret he had just left to another club to pick up some cocaine from a guitarist who kept his junk in his guitar.

Johnny went on past the Open Gate dancing-spot, past the Hostaria dell'Orso, where from the Blue Room on the first floor dimly-lit the sounds of a plaintive piano, and a melancholy songstress reached the street; and a slightly more flashy spot, the Boite Pigalle. He hurried past a restaurant called the Piccolo Budapest, where they drowned you with fiddles and balalaikas, and past La Biblioteca, a cellar-restaurant, whose walls were composed entirely of dusty wine-bottles, full, and where there was dancing to a trio which sang blue Napolitano ballads as they drifted from table to table.

When he got back to the Piazza del Gesu he discussed it with Carla who was crazy with enthusiasm about the project, and she elected to rustle up the necessary finance. That was going to be the big snag Johnny foresaw, but he was somewhat reassured by Carla's certainty that she knew where the money would be forthcoming.

Next morning Johnny walked into Transatlantic in the Piazza Colonna, the place was noisy with tourists as he went up to the counter, and bought a book of twelve hundred-dollar Transatlantic traveller's cheques. He wrote the phoney name he was using in them while the teller looked on, but with a neat touch of sleight-of-hand contrived to avoid signing the last one in the book. So he had pulled off the first part of the operation. Elated, he sauntered out of Transatlantic with a genuine unsigned traveller's cheque in the inside pocket of his navy-blue draped single-breasted jacket.

A day or two later Johnny contacted the little Englishman who had deserted from the British forces to settle in Rome and engage himself in any nefarious caper that came his way. He was known as Danny Boy, owing to a predilection for whistling snatches of the Londonderry Air between his teeth in moments of abstraction. It was a habit Danny had tried to break himself of, but he still lapsed occasionally. It would be Danny's job to take care of the creative side. And he was quite an artist in the strictly illegal way.

Meanwhile Carla had unearthed a bright-eyed Milanese, who went under the name of Giordano Trescalli. He was the front for a group who were already in the same fine, of business upon which Johnny was embarking.

The first conference took place in the Borghese Gardens, where, situated behind a black iron fence, and cut off from the rest of the rambling walks and wilderness of grass and flower-beds was a little afresco café, the Casina del Lago. The café was reached by a gravelled alley shaded by green oak trees which were delightfully cool and restful after the blazing afternoon sun. It looked like a small temple, with a small portico with classical columns, in front of which were placed little round tables and wicker chairs under the shade of vast umbrellas. Everywhere pink rhododendrons flowered out of great jars. And somewhere a radio played romantic music.

The rendezvous was Carla's choice, it was empty at certain times in the afternoon and the waiters were unobtrusive, she explained. After you had been served with your apricot ice and pink *paste* in frilled paper cups you were left alone.

And so over ices Johnny and Carla and Giordano discussed the set-up, their voices low and blurred by the radio music against any passing eavesdropper. From the tips of his shiny, pointed shoes to the lavender-coloured soft hat on his head, Giordano was strictly the old pro. Danny Boy made up the party, but he contributed little to the discussion. He wasn't much of a talker anyway. Even when Giordano scrutinized Johnny's cheque, Danny appeared to show little interest. He had seen the cheque already and had expressed his opinion on it with professional succinctness.

"This part is easy," Giordano Trescalli said with a shrug. "I know a press on which it can be run off and I know where there is plenty of paper."

"What's the problem then?" Johnny said.

Giordano looked at him with a thin smile. "The problem," he said, "is always the same problem. Where is the money to pay for all this?"

Johnny's glance flickered over Carla and then back to the other. "I thought that was your department," he said.

"Certainly I can find the cash," Giordano said. "But I want you to realize that the business-men I represent are contributing the most important part of the scheme."

Johnny's expression tightened sardonically. They were getting down to the basic fast. He had imagined there would have been a lot of chinning about the weather first. "What cut do you want?" he said.

"Fifty per cent of all the stuff that is printed," Giordano said.

Johnny thought his mouth was like a shark's snapping shut, then he glanced again at Carla and it flashed across his mind: Was she taking a cut on the side from Giordano for introducing the business? Then he eyed Danny who was sitting on the other side of him brooding over his ice-cream, which he had so far not touched.

"We will find everything," Giordano was saying. "As I said the press, and the paper. On top of which we have supplied the answer to your biggest headache, the cash to pay for it all."

"I got me my own artist," Johnny said, and he nodded towards Danny. "Don't forget that."

The other shrugged again. "The people I represent," Giordano said, "will still want fifty per cent." He glanced casually at Danny. "You can use your own engraver, provided he can do the job."

Danny raised his eyes from his ice to stare at him, and then spat expressively into the gravel path at his feet. He cracked the knuckles of his large, spatulate fingers as if to loosen them up, before contemplating his ice again.

"Okay," Johnny said.

Next day Danny took the unsigned cheque along to the small printing firm for whom he was currently working. The place was in a narrow street back of the cobbled Via Claudia, with its yellowed walls, and Danny had the run of the firm's dark-room any time he wanted. When he switched on the warning red light over the dark-room door he knew he could rely on not being interrupted for so long as the red light stayed on.

It was going to be a long job. Four plates were going to be required to give him what he wanted. One for the blue for the face of the cheque, and one for the purple on the face, another plate for the back, and another plate for the pale blue background for the cheque's serial numbers. Then there was the water-mark which was an integral part of the operation.

It turned out to be a five weeks' job, in fact. Then one evening, Danny showed up at the apartment in the Piazza del Gesu with the requisite plates, casually wrapped in bits of cloth and old newspaper. A little while after his arrival in the large comfortable living-room that looked out over the roofs and upper storeys of Rome silhouetted against the pale blues and pinks of the evening sky, shadowed eternally by the sweeping flocks of swifts and the plates had met with Johnny's approval, Carla showed up with Giordano. The outcome of the discussion which followed was the Italian's somewhat reluctant agreement that Danny had done an artistic job, and an arrangement to meet next afternoon with those who were to be responsible for printing the counterfeit cheques.

Chapter Three

THE BUSINESS-MEN for whom Giordano Trescalli was the front operated from a little pasticcerie behind the railway-station by the east wall of the city. Among their hangers-on was a man who owned a London-made Rotaprint offset press that had found its way into Italy before the war to become diverted from its original legitimate purpose. Now it was for hire for a fee, no questions asked, to anyone who cared to hire it.

The owner of the press kept it in a backyard shack, and whoever wanted to use it had to move it from the shack and set the press up for himself. While Danny Boy had been busily exercising his artistic talents working direct on to the finely grained surface of the thin, aluminium plates, Johnny and Giordano had contacted an ex-stick-up artist who now ran a small coffee-bar on the city's outskirts, where the Ponte Milvio carried the Great North Road out of Rome.

The ex-stick-up artist rented the cellar for three weeks for thirty thousand lira, and a couple of days before Danny had arrived at the Piazza del Gesu with the completed plates, a truck carrying the Rotaprint under wraps and Johnny and Giordano pulled up outside the coffee-bar. Discreetly the proprietor made himself scarce, while the two others unloaded the press, sundry paper and containers of ink, and transferred them down into the cellar.

Over the course of the next three weeks Danny, sometimes accompanied by Johnny or Giordano, or both, would appear at the coffee-bar, surreptitiously descend into the cellar, and lock the door behind them. Presently the sound of the offset would be heard. In the early stages Johnny watched fascinated as Danny operated the machine, the plate cylinder turning and the rubber blanket of the blanket cylinder transferring the ink from the plate to the paper as it passed between the blanket and the impression cylinder. Danny had faked the watermark so brilliantly that the planchettes appeared to have been built right into the paper during its manufacture, as they were in the genuine cheques, instead of in fact being merely drawn on the plate and printed.

"How many will you knock off from these plates?" Johnny asked Danny. "I mean how long will the plate last, before they get blurred?"

"They'll stay sharp long enough for this job," Danny said cryptically, "and longer."

Johnny nodded thoughtfully, he was wondering what happened to the plates after Danny had finished with this particular operation. Danny was banging on the ceiling above with the end of a broomstick, and soon the cellar-door was opened barely wide enough for coffee and sandwiches to be pushed through. Danny often worked on through the night, snatching an hour or two's sleep on the floor.

Late one evening, when Johnny and Danny were below, Giordano arrived at the coffee-bar with the truck. He paid the landlord his thirty thousand lira, and advised him to keep his attention strictly to the business of his own coffee-bar, while the press was wrapped up once more, lugged upstairs, heaved aboard the truck and returned quietly to its owner.

On the Rotaprint Danny had during three weeks underground produced six thousand counterfeit hundred dollar Transatlantic travellers' cheques.

Now the caper had reached its most critical phase. The counterfeits were actually in existence, and the big risk was that the police might hear about them through the underworld grapevine, before the first counterfeit was cashed. Even if that danger was avoided, Johnny and the rest of them knew precisely what would happen within a week or so after the first cheque was put on the market. Transatlantic would learn it was a counterfeit, and would alert all its branches and every bank in Europe. Bank-tellers who had previously honoured Transatlantic travellers' cheques without a second glance would henceforth scrutinize every one that came before them with gimlet eyes. Hotel-cashiers, airport ticket-clerks, jewellers — all those who handled large sums of money would become suspicious-minded to a morbid degree.

What it amounted to was that Johnny and Giordano's mob would in fact have little more than a couple of weeks at best in which to unload the stuff. It would be every man for himself, and Johnny suddenly realized that Giordano and his pals stood a better chance of unloading than he did.

The delivery of the six thousand travellers' cheques took place in the workroom of a dim theatrical costumiers owned by a friend of Carla's. Johnny, accompanied by Danny, who was tottering under the weight of a bulky valise, appeared at this musty, cluttered rendezvous next day at midday following the departure of the Rotaprint from the coffee-bar cellar, Giordano and Carla were awaiting them.

Danny heaved the suitcase on to a table, squashing a couple of tinselled head-dresses all out of shape, Johnny lifting the lid of the valise to allow Giordano a tantalizing glimpse of the contents, now indicated his readiness to hand over the fifty per cent due to Giordano and his business-men he represented in a week's time and not before. He wanted the extra time in order to get rid of his stuff before the others went into action.

Giordano took a poor view of the suggestion, and was vehemently backed up by Carla, not much to Johnny's surprise, he had suspected for the past few weeks that Carla was cheating on him with Giordano. Danny, as usual, said nothing. He merely stood there regarding his spatulate fingers, without whose delicate skill there wouldn't have been the six thousand cheques to start with.

After a good deal of chinning, during which no one changed anyone's viewpoint, Giordano said he would have to consult with his business-men, and would be back with their answer in an hour. Johnny agreed to hang around and the other, accompanied by Carla, her dark eyes flashing dangerously at Johnny, departed.

Giordano and Carla duly returned, the former to announce that he had induced the business-men he represented to make Johnny a counter-proposal which was to let him have an extra thousand of the cheques for himself in consideration of the happy relationship he and Johnny had enjoyed. But both parties must start getting rid of the stuff together. This was very, very definite.

Johnny finally agreed, and he and Danny transferred the requisite number of cheques from valise to the hatboxes provided by Carla's friend, and he and Danny who carried the valise, said *arivederla* to Giordano and Carla and beat it.

That night Johnny and Danny took a plane of one of the sixty-six airlines serving Rome and lit out for Antwerp. Working fast and moving around, they spread the counterfeits all over Belgium, some of the stuff was to appear even as far afield as Scandinavia, Germany and Austria, Czechoslovakia and Switzerland.

But what Johnny hadn't known was that at the very time that Danny was toiling away beneath the coffee-bar another bunch of counterfeiters had moved into the picture. This crowd had, a few weeks before, dreamed up an ambitious plan for faking fifty-dollar counterfeit Transatlantic travellers' cheques to be followed by twenties and then tens. One of this mob's contacts, an individual known as the Lizard, was instructed to locate a supply of paper. Among the first people he talked to was Giordano, an old acquaintance.

The Lizard thus reported back that a counterfeit hundred-dollar cheque was already being printed. Accordingly, his confederates decided it would be safer and simpler to get in on the Johnny Destiny set-up instead of going through with their own scheme. The Lizard came back to Giordano and told him that in view of what was already planned, his friends had dropped their own idea.

But, the Lizard said, if Giordano needed any help over disposing of the cheques, his crowd had an outlet in mind which would buy an almost unlimited amount. As a result Giordano accompanied by Carla, had met the Lizard's boss. He was a Frenchman from Nice, whose clothes were impeccably tailored, whose manners were charming, and who used a violet scent profusely.

Two nights following this meeting in Rome, Johnny and Danny walked into the hotel in Brussels, where the pair had arrived that afternoon. In the train, earlier, Johnny had been overcome with a premonition that something nasty was due to overtake him. So insistent was this foreboding that he felt impelled to remove a fistful of counterfeit cheques from the valise while Danny was obliviously asleep in the railway compartment and transfer them to his own suitcase.

And it was the same foreboding which caused him to allow Danny, carrying the suitcase, to precede him by several yards as they went into the hotel-entrance.

So that when two men, obviously plainclothes detectives, stepped from behind a cigarette-kiosk in the crowded foyer and grabbed Danny firmly by both arms, while at the same time taking possession of the valise, Johnny was not too overcome with shock to spin on his heel and make a dash for it. "We have got you with the stuff on you," he had time to hear one of the police-officers say to Danny in mangled English, and then he was dodging the traffic in the busy street.

Johnny was not to know that one of the plain-clothes-men was an ex-police inspector, who had been sacked sometime before for black market activities, and that his companion was an officer still in the force, but not long destined to serve in his present employment. Danny was carted off, not to any police-station, but to a café, where upon a pretext he was left, while the two others departed, the valise with them, due to find its way into the hands of the Lizard's boss in Rome.

It was ten days later that Transatlantic realized that a counterfeit hundred-dollar traveller's cheque had been put into circulation in Rome; followed within only a few hours by a report arrived from Brussels that a man had actually showed up on the Bourse with a Transatlantic hundred dollar cheque but had vanished when told it was a fake. Next day the police in Rome picked up four characters who were attempting to buy jewellery with one of the counterfeits, and who were found to have twenty more duds in their possession. The same afternoon a man was arrested in a café on the Champs-Elysées while attempting to sell ten of the counterfeits to a detective over an aperitif.

During the next three weeks it became painfully clear to Transatlantic and the police that the counterfeiters were really putting their hearts into their work. Bogus cheques were turning up all over Western Europe. A Lucerne bank refused to cash one of them for an unknown brunette, whereupon she beat a retreat, not staying to pick up the cheque in her haste; the same day several of them arrived at Transatlantic's clearing-house in New York; a man was arrested in Basle with seven of them in his possession, which he said he had come by in Strasbourg.

The Banque de France reported that it had received forty-eight of the counterfeits which had been confiscated by customs officers two days previously at Vallorbe, on the Swiss border. The traveller had, contrary to currency regulations, not declared the cheques which was why they had been confiscated; the customs men not realizing that they were counterfeit, had let the man who was carrying them through into Switzerland. His passport had borne the name: James Donnell, of Detroit.

It was in fact, Johnny Destiny.

Coincidentally, in view of certain events that lay in wait around the corner of the not-too-distant future, it was at this time that Dr. Morelle chanced to arrive in Rome from Paris, with two friends who happened to be ace counterfeiting experts, Commissaire Principal Yves Altmeyer, of the Paris police, and Commissaire Principal Paul Roland, of the Surete Nationale. Dr. Morelle was attending a conference of international criminologists and Interpol police-officers.

Pounced upon by news-hawks for his opinion upon the Transatlantic sensation, Dr. Morelle gave it as his opinion that the source of the counterfeits was Rome, and that, therefore, all of those picked up by the police so far were very likely to be only peddlers, not the actual counterfeiters themselves.

Later, at Rome police-headquarters one of the chief detectives engaged on the case asked Dr. Morelle for his reason behind the statement he had given the newspaper reporters. Dr. Morelle indicated several of the counterfeit cheques which lay on the wide office-desk before him. "I saw some of these in Paris," he said, "in Commissaire Principal Roland's dossier. The serial number was the same. I recall that it is the serial number used for all travellers' cheques issued by Transatlantic office in this city."

It took six months to prove Dr. Morelle right, when the net finally closed round Giordano Trescalli, his business-men crowd, and the Lizard mob. Carla was one who contrived to wriggle through the meshes, so did the charming Frenchman, user of the violet scent. Two other fish who contrived to remain free were Danny Boy and Johnny Destiny.

Slipping back from Switzerland and into France, Johnny had gone to ground for a while in Marseilles; then he had drifted along the Cote d'Azur, until he had landed up in Vichy. It was a certain item of news he had picked up at the Grand Casino one evening which had brought a sudden gleam into his pale eyes. Next day he had taken a hired Simca Versailles and headed for Paris.

As he hustled the car through the old town of Billy, its medieval castle crumbling on top of the hill, and then along La Route Bleu, his mind was running before him, full of the big idea that had struck him.

This notion, it had come to him right out of nothing. Johnny Destiny smiled thinly to himself as his foot squeezed down harder on the gas.

Chapter Four

JOHNNY DESTINY HAD booked a room at the hotel off the Rue de Dunkerque, near the Gare du Nord, from which he would be leaving for London early next morning. But when he arrived in Paris in the late evening and drove to the hotel, he found inexplicably that no one behind Reception knew anything about him. The place was full and there wasn't a room for him.

Irritated by the hotel's muddling, and dismissing the thought which emerged from the back of his mind that this was an unlucky omen, Johnny marched out snarling to find accommodation elsewhere. It took him half-an-hour driving round, from the Madeline to the Place de la Bastille, from the Rue de Rivoli to the Champs-Elysées, before he eventually wound up at the Hotel Scribe.

He phoned the car-hire company to pick up the Simca as prearranged with the Vichy office, and then he went out for a drink at Georges Carpentier's bar, where he sat and watched the tourists strolling by, and the window-shoppers out for a saunter. The summer night was warm but there was a cool breeze off the Seine, which filled Johnny with the exhilaration he remembered from his last visit to Paris way back at the end of the war.

He looked in at the Café de la Paix for a brief while, keeping a watchful eye against running into someone who might recognize him from Rome or even the old days in Germany. But there was no one; then he went back to his hotel for a steak Chateaubriand and half a bottle of Vin Rose and then sat out in the foyer over coffee and a smooth cognac.

He began to feel sleepy, the long drive from Vichy along the banks of the River Loire had tired him more than he thought. After admiring the jewellery and gold wrist-watches in the hotel's show-case, Johnny left instructions to be called. "*Reveillez-moi a six heures*," and he went upstairs to his room.

He took a leisurely bath, all the time his mind full of the idea that had sparked his trip to Paris. He lay in bed mulling it over, weighing the risks and chances, his pale eyes gleaming at the prospect of the profits and the yen to be back in the big-time once again, and then suddenly he was asleep.

Half-past six next morning he stood outside the hotel, gripping his small suitcase, waiting for the taxi that had been ordered to take him to the Gare du Nord. The taxi appeared and he was speeding through the Paris streets, with the workers streaming off the buses and the Metro, and hazy with a summer morning mist. Then the taxi was pulling up outside the grimy, barracks-like station.

He found the train for Calais relatively empty; and as the outskirts of Paris gave way to the rolling landscape which was beginning to wilt already under the brazen sky, Johnny browsed through the English and American newspapers he had bought in Paris. Presently Amiens Cathedral was receding into the distant blue and the train was speeding through Abbeville, then the pale khaki sand-dunes and Paris Plage; next Boulogne and then Calais Maritime.

It was just on midday when he boarded the steamer, with the sun beating down on the brass and white paint of the decks. He went below and left his suitcase in the smoking-room, then up on deck again to watch abstractedly the activity on the dock-side, the gulls swooping round the vessel, and diving to the debris that floated on the shining surface of the water. Presently with deep tremulous sighs the steamer swung away from the quayside, and headed out of the harbour, beyond the sand-dunes, to where the sea lay flat and glaring.

Without a backward glance at Calais, Johnny went below for lunch. The boat appeared about half-full of passengers, and Johnny found a table to himself in the restaurant.

It was several years since he had paid a brief visit to London, he was thinking, as he gave his order to the hatchet-faced waiter with a cockney accent. That was in the Hamburg days and he had flown over for a long weekend. It had been winter and his impression of London in the daytime was that it was dark and raining. Not that he'd seen much of London by day, he knew most about it at night, the night-clubs and restaurants. And the night-clubs were like any other night-clubs anywhere else in the world, only they clipped you in an English accent.

He was glancing out of the port at the brilliance of the sky and thinking that London in summer mightn't be so bad, when a girl's voice brought his attention round to a slim young woman who was standing at his table.

"Do you mind if I sit here?" she was saying to him. She was a brunette with a warm smile and a calm expression in her grey eyes. She was wearing a neat summery frock and her bare arms were only lightly tanned.

As Johnny nodded, he glanced round the restaurant and observed that although it was not very full, all the tables round about him, were occupied by at least one passenger.

"Go right ahead," he said.

With a smile of thanks she sat down and began ordering her lunch. The girl made only monosyllabic replies to the one or two chummy observations Johnny put in, and he decided she was a typical English type, cold and standoffish and not given to talking to strangers, once the topic of the weather had been exhausted. She had only one course and then asked for coffee which she had with milk. Johnny was finishing his cup of black coffee and smoking a cigarette. He offered her his packet.

"Like American cigarettes?"

She took one with a little smile and he noticed that she had nice teeth.

"I do as a matter of fact," she said. "Though I don't smoke them very often. Not that I smoke at all very much."

He lit her cigarette for her with the gold Cartier lighter he had bought in Rome and noticed her gaze linger on it in his lean sunburnt hand.

"It's the French ones I can't stand," she said, as she drew appreciatively at her cigarette. "They're so terribly strong."

"You get used to them," he said.

"They say you can get used to anything," she said with a little laugh.

He grinned at her. "For my money," he said, "Paris wouldn't be the same without the French cigarettes' scent."

"Do you know Paris well?" she said.

"Not so well," he said. "I suppose I was really thinking of the other places I know, like Marseilles or Nice, which wouldn't be the same either, without the smell of French cigarettes."

They sat for about twenty minutes talking in a desultory way. The cigarette seemed to make the girl relax, as she told Johnny how she was on her way back to London after a week in Paris. It was her first time there, and she said that in a way she would have liked to have stayed on for the other week remaining of her holiday, only she had made arrangements which she couldn't change. She was going down to an aunt in Essex, she said.

When she got up from the table, Johnny stood up, and together they went up from the coolness below on deck into the bright sunshine. Already the French coastline had disappeared from view and ahead of them glinted a hint of chalky-white on the horizon. They were standing against the side of the vessel on the upper deck. The girl was breathing in gulps of sea air while Johnny narrowed his gaze absently at the dazzling sea.

"Do you know that man?" the girl said suddenly. And Johnny's head came up with a jerk to meet her grey eyes with a quizzical glance.

"What man?"

He hadn't turned his head, looking beyond her shoulder he could see only a middle-aged couple talking quietly together, and beyond them an elderly man, whose back was towards him.

"Don't look now," she said, "but he's just behind you. He's been staring at you for the past minute. I wondered if he knew you."

He shook his head. A warning bell rang at the back of his mind, a question-mark of danger formed out of his thoughts. There was always the chance of this, of someone he didn't want should recognize him from way back when he'd gone A.W.O.L., for example, doing just that thing. He didn't turn his head yet. It was the risk he had to take. He figured it was unlikely at that. He'd changed quite a bit the past few years. His body had thickened, he was more jowly about the face, there was plenty of grey around the temples and the nape of his neck. His skin was very dark, burnt by the sun of the South of France.

"I think he was having lunch at the same time that we were," she was saying.

"I guess it's you he's looking at, not me." Still he didn't turn his head.

But she shook her head. "He looks rather like you, as a matter of fact. He's turned away now," she said. "Perhaps he guessed I was talking about him."

Now, slowly, casually, Johnny turned to look at the man. He was leaning against part of the ship's superstructure, his gaze now out to sea. He was thick-set, in his late thirty's Johnny calculated, and, yes, he figured, there could be a kind of resemblance between them. His skin through which the beard showed round his chin was burnt dark by the sun. By the cut of his suit, Johnny concluded that he was an American, too.

Johnny didn't recognize him, so far as he knew he'd never seen the man before. He turned back to the girl.

"Looks like he's an American," he said. "Maybe he heard my accent, and he was interested in there being another American around."

The girl seemed to accept this explanation, though Johnny thought he caught a hint of perplexity in the look she threw beyond him. "He's stopped looking at you now, anyway," she said. "In fact, he's walking away."

Johnny didn't turn to glance after the other man. He offered the girl another of his cigarettes, but she shook her head. Johnny took one himself, and cupped the flame of his lighter with his hand as he lit it. He dragged at it deeply, feeling vaguely disturbed, by the thought of the man walking away behind him. He knew for sure it was no one he knew, his memory for faces was all right. It always had been. But that couldn't mean it wasn't someone who, even if they hadn't been socially introduced, had seen him some place, and knew who he was.

On the other hand, it could mean nothing. Just, like he had said, another Yank hearing him talking and giving him the casual once-over out of curiosity. No more to it than that.

The man didn't reappear, and Johnny didn't go in search of him, there was nothing to be gained by that. Presently the gulls gleaming white in the sunlight of the early afternoon were screaming round the decks as the steamer eased its way into Folkestone harbour. The girl had quit Johnny's side earlier to check her luggage, leaving him to gaze speculatively at the chalky cliffs and green of the downs that rose above the little town, beyond the quayside buildings.

He didn't see the girl again, though he looked out for her casually when he himself went below to pick up his own suitcase. He kept an eye peeled for the man, but didn't spot him in the bustle of disembarkation.

So he was through the Customs, after a perfunctory examination and on to Folkestone harbour platform, walking along beside the train due to leave shortly for London. Like the steamer, the train was only half-full, and Johnny found a first-class compartment to himself. Putting his suitcase on the rack he got out of the compartment and stood on the platform, still looking casually for the brunette, still wondering if he'd see the man on the boat.

But she wasn't anywhere to be seen, and he decided that she must have got ashore well ahead of him, he hadn't hurried and she was by now somewhere on the train. The man didn't show up either.

The platform-clock said half-past four and the train was pulling out and Johnny went along to the restaurant car for a drink. He threw a glance at the compartments he passed, but there was no girl, no man. Nor did he glimpse either of them in the restaurant-car.

It was sometime later when he was back in his compartment, glancing idly through a glossy magazine he had bought on the station bookstall. The compartment-door slid open and Johnny glanced up over his magazine. It was the man the girl had pointed out to him on the steamer.

He closed the door behind him, and sat down in the corner diagonally opposite Johnny. He didn't say anything. He didn't even glance in Johnny's direction.

Chapter Five

AT APPROXIMATELY THE same time that Johnny Destiny went aboard the cross-channel steamer at Calais, the telephone rang in the study at 221b Harley Street, London. Miss Frayle, who had been sitting with her pencil flying over a note-book taking down Dr. Morelle's dictation, picked up the receiver. A man's voice answered her, he sounded as if he was choking. "Roses — those roses —"

"What?" Miss Frayle said, her eyes wide.

"It's a bowl of roses," the man gasped painfully. "The scent — I can't get my breath —"

"Who is that?" Miss Frayle asked quickly.

"It's Mr. Beaumont — tell Dr. Morelle —"

His voice rasped her ear in another fit of choking as Miss Frayle turned to Dr. Morelle, who had not glanced up from the notes on his desk in which he was absorbed. But now he shot a look from under his dark brows at the telephone-receiver she held.

"Mr. Beaumont," Miss Frayle said, answering his unspoken query. "He sounds rather ill —"

Dr. Morelle had crossed to her swiftly and he took the telephone. "Dr. Morelle here."

"I'm choking to death, Doctor — this asthma. Someone put roses on the table in my sitting-room, and —"

"Did you take the adrenalin injection I prescribed for you?"

"Yes, yes — but it doesn't help. I've got to see you."

There followed another fit of coughing, and Dr. Morelle instructed the other to get into a taxi and proceed to Harley Street as quickly as he could. When Dr. Morelle had replaced the receiver, Miss Frayle said: "Poor Mr. Beaumont, what causes this asthma, Doctor?"

"It is a spasmodic condition of the bronchi, that is the two windpipes that lead to the lungs. The patient is unable to exhale the dead air, and feels that he is suffocating."

Miss Frayle was looking puzzled. "How could roses have given him asthma? I mean, they're such lovely flowers."

"The symbol of love, eh, Miss Frayle?"

"I wasn't thinking of them in that way."

"Never mind, so long as you think of them."

Miss Frayle blinked at him over her spectacles. "What do you mean?"

"I want you to hurry out and buy some roses."

"Roses, Dr. Morelle?" Miss Frayle beamed, blushing slightly. "For me?"

"Get them from Finlayson's in Oxford Street." "Finlayson's? But, Doctor —"

"Three dozen red roses, which to you symbolize love and romance, but which to Beaumont symbolize suffocation. Come along, don't stand there gaping at me, I require them before Mr. Beaumont arrives."

Miss Frayle had returned to Harley Street only a few minutes from the curious errand upon which Dr. Morelle had dispatched her, when the front doorbell rang. It was as she expected the asthmatic patient. He was a youngish man, wearing a well-cut suit, and his face above his dark, subdued tie was a rather greyish tinge, with shadows under his eyes.

"Dr. Morelle's waiting for you, Mr. Beaumont. I do hope you're feeling better."

"Yes, thanks. But I really thought I'd had it that time."

Miss Frayle led the way to Dr. Morelle's study. She opened the door and closed it again on Beaumont and Dr. Morelle who stood negligently leaning against his desk. His visitor took a step towards him and then his eyes dilated, his jaw dropped, and he indicated the desk as Dr. Morelle moved away from it.

"Those roses —" he gasped and went into a paroxysm of coughing, a shaking hand pointed at the bowl, full of red roses, dark red, deep pink and glorious crimson roses.

"Miss Frayle must have put them there, most careless of her," Dr. Morelle said urbanely.

"I can't breathe — the scent — I'm choking. Give me a shot of adrenalin —"

Dr. Morelle calmly moved aside from the bowl of roses on his desk, behind which was the macabre-looking human skull which served as a cigarette-box. The veins in Beaumont's forehead swelled, and he looked as if he would suffocate. "I'll give you a hypodermic," Dr. Morelle said. "Let's see, you've refused to have any skin-tests. You said you'd had some before you came to me?"

Beaumont nodded and quickly unfastened his gold cufflink and proceeded to push his shirt-sleeve high up his arm. His fingers were trembling in his agitation, his brow was moist with perspiration. The hypodermic flashed in the sunlight that streamed in through the window as Dr. Morelle picked it up in readiness to administer the injection. Dr. Morelle bent over the bare forearm. In a moment it was over. "Now try and relax," he said to the other.

Beaumont was already looking better, some colour had found its way to his cheekbones. "That's better," he said, more calmly. "I really thought I was for the high jump."

"Death, a necessary end, will come when it will come," was Dr. Morelle's reply.

Beaumont was shaking his head with disbelief. "But how did you come to leave those roses there, when you were expecting me?"

"I must reprimand Miss Frayle for her carelessness. According to her they symbolize romance. Look at this one —"

"No, really — I," Beaumont said. "Why, why, it's made of paper —"

"Precisely. A paper rose. They're all paper roses. Miss Frayle has just brought them back from a shop in Oxford Street. Very realistic, don't you think?"

"Paper roses — not real roses at all," said Beaumont. "No more than the adrenalin in the hypodermic injection. It was merely sterilized distilled water."

"Water?"

"Paper roses and water," Dr. Morelle said.

"What are you getting at?"

"It means that your asthma attacks are the result not of an allergy to roses, they are caused by a neurosis. A fear of something you are afraid to reveal." The other was staring at him as if he were a creature from another planet. It was an expression in the faces of his patients and many people who encountered him to which Dr. Morelle was not altogether unaccustomed. "The next step, accordingly, is to discover what it is of which you are afraid."

A few minutes later, Beaumont now completely relaxed was talking easily and quickly. "It was seven or eight weeks ago, Dr. Morelle," he was saying. "I'd gone up to my father's bedroom. He wasn't there, the bathroom-door was open and quite by chance I glanced in, and there he was in the bath. He had slipped and hit his head. I started to pull him out, and then this extraordinary sensation came over me." He broke off and bit his lip, his brows drawn together in a dark frown.

"An overwhelming compulsion to leave him as he was?" Dr. Morelle said. "Was that what you were about to say?"

The other nodded and went on. "Everything flashed in my mind, the overpowering knowledge that his will was in my favour, and that by leaving him I wouldn't really be guilty of murdering him —"

"But in fact, you dragged him out of the bath?"

Again a nod. "I carried him into the bedroom and within a few minutes he'd recovered and was perfectly all right. I left a couple of hours later and got a taxi home." He paused and glanced at Dr. Morelle as if he was arriving at the most impressive part of his story. "I hadn't been in the taxi long," he said slowly, "when I noticed the scent of roses. It became so overpowering that I had to stop the taxi. In the corner was a bunch of roses. Must have been left there by a previous passenger. By now I was almost choking to death, and I had to get another taxi to take me home." His voice fell away to a whisper. "I — I'm afraid I've not been very frank with you," he said.

Dr. Morelle was leaning forward, his brilliant gaze transfixing him. "This was the first asthmatic attack you ever suffered? And which you attributed to the roses?"

"Yes, that first attack passed off, but that night I couldn't sleep. I kept on realizing how near death Father had been, and it would have been my fault."

"Plus your subconscious realization," Dr. Morelle said, "that his will played an important part in the circumstances."

"You see, sometimes he decides that he'll leave everything to me. Then he changes his mind and leaves it all to his sister. Then he'll decide to leave half to us each. It's a joke, except there's nothing very funny about being left £20,000."

"And even less amusing not to be left it," Dr. Morelle said. "Are you a frequent visitor to your father's house?"

"I'm always in and out," Beaumont said. "My flat's only the other side of Regent's Park. He's pretty lonely, hardly anyone else goes to see him."

"And," Dr. Morelle said, "your motive for giving this somewhat eccentric old man the pleasure of your company would be purely disinterested?"

31

The other was visibly confused and then he answered hesitantly. "Er — yes," he said.

"You have made it clear," Dr. Morelle said, his tone rasping, "that you might inherit a large sum of money upon your father's death. Obviously you are profoundly inhibited by the prospect. Up till now you have proved an unresponsive patient, hence the strategem I perpetrated upon you with the paper roses; having, as a result, come this far, don't hold out at the last."

"I might as well confess it, Dr. Morelle."

"Confession is good for the soul." Dr. Morelle lit one of his inevitable Le Sphinx.

"I've had a rough time this last couple of years," Beaumont said. "I may not be flat broke, but I'm damn near it."

"So that your visits to your father are quite calculated?"

"I suppose you might say so."

The man facing him sank his head as Dr. Morelle said: "There is precious little supposition about it; you are striving your utmost to remain in his affections in the hope that you will benefit by his death."

"In my secret heart, yes."

"It is into your secret heart that we are probing. There lie your subconscious guilt-complexes, your obsessive delusion that roses give you asthma."

"What can I do to help myself?"

"You have already achieved much by at last understanding the truth about your asthmatic symptoms," Dr. Morelle said, "and the truth about yourself. My advice is to concentrate your mind upon using your talents to remedy your financial situation. Come and see me again in two weeks' time, and tell me what plans you have made to make yourself independent of your father's capricious eccentricities."

"I see what you mean, Dr. Morelle."

It was at this point that Miss Frayle came in, Dr. Morelle turned to her. "Mr. Beaumont is just going, he'll be ringing up for an appointment in a fortnight. When you will have returned from your holiday."

"Yes, Dr. Morelle." Miss Frayle smiled at Beaumont, noting the decided improvement in his appearance. His eyes were brighter, his complexion less palid, there was a briskness about his demeanour.

"Thanks, Doctor," Beaumont was saying. "Thanks so much for all you've done. I promise you I'll try and sort myself out."

And Miss Frayle gently urged him out into the hall towards the front door. There were occasions, rare though they might be, when Miss Frayle permitted a certain amount of self-interest to deflect her preoccupation with the interests of Dr. Morelle and his patients. This was one of them.

She had a train to catch.

Chapter Six

MISS FRAYLE CAME out of the tube-exit at Victoria Station and, dodging through the crowd that milled about her into the brief tunnel, turned left. Her eyes behind her horn-rimmed glasses fastened at once on the big whitefaced clock suspended high above the perspiring holiday throngs and hurrying porters, and she checked her time with her wrist-watch.

She was all right. More than ten minutes before the train was due to arrive and here she was, the platform bang in front of her, with the words Golden Arrow arched over the gates. She glanced at the Continental Arrivals indicator, which advised her that the twenty-four hour system for railway times operated on the Continent, therefore she must subtract twelve from the figure shown. It was a form of mathematics with which she was not entirely unfamiliar, yet somehow it never failed to fluster her.

The time of the arrival of the boat-train from Folkestone was shown as 16.05. Five minutes past four, that would be, and she glanced at the clock again and then at her wrist-watch. Nothing was said that the boat-train would not be arriving on time and she looked about her with a relaxed smile of anticipation.

Her eyes caught the other train indicator nearby, and the magic names: Orient Express, Zurich, Zagreb, Warsaw. Her imagination was fired with pictures of romantic places seen from luxurious railway-compartment windows, or from the softly-lit table of a restaurant-car speeding through a purple twilight sprinkled like stars with the lights of glamorous cities, and around her the aroma of cigars and exotic scents of dark, svelte women with foreign-looking eyes.

Miss Frayle gave a little sigh. She often thought how wonderful it would be to spend a holiday on a train like the Orient Express. Still, dreams were dreams, but in reality she was just about to begin her holiday, which while it mightn't take her across Europe was going to be most enjoyable, she felt sure.

She took a platform-ticket from the machine by the barrier. Everything had gone smoothly since she had left Dr. Morelle at Harley Street just after lunch. Allowing herself plenty of time, she had taken her suitcase by taxi to Liverpool Street and deposited it in the station cloakroom. Then she took the tube to Victoria Station, and here she was, going onto platform eight to meet Erica Travers off the boat-train from Folkestone. Together they would take a taxi to Liverpool Street in time to have a cup of tea before catching the 5.12 to Sharbridge, in Essex, where Miss Frayle was going to spend two weeks' holiday aboard the houseboat owned by Erica's aunt.

Two weeks away from hot, noisy London, the dust and the crowds along Oxford Street, the buses and angry taxis in Piccadilly. Two weeks away from the typewriter and dictaphone in the study at 221b Harley Street, the telephone and the doorbell, the patients and the dossiers, the filing-cabinets and the microscopes, the gleaming test-tubes and the specimen-jars of the laboratory. Two weeks away from Dr. Morelle.

Miss Frayle's heart felt light, her blue eyes sparkled as her imagination filled with the mental pictures she had been conjuring up of the houseboat on the creek which Erica Travers had described to her so enthusiastically before she had gone off to Paris.

"It's out of this world in every sense of the term," Erica had said. "Nothing to do, except laze about in the sun all day. Swimming and sunbathing, eating and sleeping. Nothing to think of, nothing to worry about."

Miss Frayle had never been to Essex before, at least not to stay for any time at all, but she had been fascinated by Erica's description of the creeks and marshes, the saltings teeming with wildfowl and the quaint, isolated villages with their picturesque boarded houses. A world of its own, on its own, which had managed to remain unspoilt to a great extent by the advance of urban civilization, a world uninvaded by despoiling holiday-crowds, charabancs and streams of cars, choking the quiet roads.

"That's what's such bliss," Erica had said, "it's so marvellously inaccessible. Something to be said for a rotten train-service, and the trains to that part are ghastly, but it does save us from the mob."

Erica Travers was secretary to a research biologist working at the Welbeck Hospital. Miss Frayle had met her quite a lot during the past several months: Dr. Morelle had been using the wonderfully equipped laboratory at the Welbeck for some of his more advanced experimental work, in which he had been assisted by Erica's boss; and Erica and Miss Frayle, teaming-up on their respective employers' behalf, had often lunched together at a little restaurant in Marylebone High Street which Erica had discovered, and had become good friends.

Erica was a few years younger than Miss Frayle, but was self-possessed and poised and with a confident air which seemed to suit her smart, brunette good looks. It was she who had inspired Miss Frayle with the idea of spending her two weeks' holiday with Erica and her aunt in Essex on the houseboat, *Moya*. At least it wouldn't work out quite like that. Erica herself was taking her holiday a week earlier than Miss Frayle, and had already planned to split her own fortnight into two parts, the first week in Paris, which she had always longed to visit, followed by the second week with her aunt in Essex. So the idea had developed that Miss Frayle should spend her first week's holiday on the houseboat with Erica, during the latter's last week, and then stay on for the remaining week after Erica had returned to London.

"If you want to, that is of course," Erica Travers had said. "After all, you may not like it. But if you're bored there are several places nearby where I'm sure you could be put up for the rest of your holiday. I mean, I suppose Aunt is a bit eccentric, and you may find her too much to cope with on your own. Personally, I adore her."

That was the arrangement, although Miss Frayle felt quite certain she would find Erica's aunt easy enough to get along with. She looked forward to spending the remaining week on the houseboat, in her company.

Miss Frayle was smiling a little to herself as she moved along the platform, awaiting the boat-train's arrival. She was anticipating how full Erica would be of her week in Paris. Miss Frayle felt quite blasé about it, she had accompanied Dr. Morelle to Paris on several occasions in the past when he had gone there in the course of his work. True, her stay each time had been of only a brief duration, Erica had spent an entire week there, and on her own, free to roam Paris and enjoy it without any ties of work.

The platform was not very crowded. Miss Frayle found it almost restful and felt thankful that she did not have to wait where the long queues and noisy travellers bustled and eddied about, desperately bent on getting away from hot, sticky London for the holiday coasts.

Then her rising anticipation as the moment of the train's arrival drew near was tinged by a sudden feeling of guilt. Involuntarily she had let her mind fly back to 221b Harley Street, and the study where she had left Dr. Morelle. She was recollecting how the last she had seen of him was his tall angular back as he stood apparently absorbed in the view from the window of the sky above the house-tops.

She recalled with a distinct pang the distant chilliness of his tone in contrast to hers when she had said good-bye. He had barely responded, certainly he had abstained from wishing her a happy holiday. She had glanced into the laboratory with its glint of glass and chromium, its ordered shelves and benches, just to reassure herself that everything was in order, and then looked round the familiar booklined study and its files of dossiers. She had stared again at the tall black silhouette, still turned uncompromisingly, back towards her, then with a shrug of her slim shoulders Miss Frayle hurried out into Harley Street.

She recalled now with a faint wry smile how in her haste she had let the front door slam with a crash which seemed to have shaken the house, and in her mind's eye she could visualize the expression on Dr. Morelle's gaunt features as that door-slam echoed in the study where he stood.

Then Miss Frayle shook off the shadow that threatened to stretch out from Harley Street and darken her ebullient spirits and resolutely she looked forward again to the next two weeks of escape from that hooded, piercing gaze, those sardonic tones and that driving energy, that dominating personality. Two weeks of lazing in the sun, swimming and sunbathing. She smiled again to herself, remembering the swimsuit she had bought herself. An elegant item in the latest style, and which she intended to make good use of during the next couple of weeks.

There was a surge of movement around her as the straggle of porters and passengers began moving past; and she saw the train curve into sight at the end of the stretched-out platform, and straighten itself out as it snaked towards her. The boat-train from Folkestone arriving on the dot.

Eagerly Miss Frayle joined the movement of the rest of the people on the platform, and as the train's speed slackened, began searching for Erica. The carriages moved more slowly past, and then suddenly she caught sight of her leaning out excitedly from a window.

"Erica." And Miss Frayle hurried forward as Erica Travers called out and waved to her. She saw at once how well the other was looking, and in the same moment noticed that she was wearing a sleeveless frock of what appeared to her to be unmistakably Parisian cut. Trust dear Erica, she thought amusedly, and wondered how much of her week's salary that had cost her. No doubt she would soon hear all about it. Just a few thousand francs, absolutely irresistible, simply couldn't refuse a bargain like it, my first real Paris frock.

The train gasped to a halt, carriage-doors swung wide, and Miss Frayle was helping Erica out of the compartment with her two suitcases, taking one herself, while Erica held the other, and shaking their heads at a would-be helpful porter who appeared out of the tangle of passengers and those meeting them, crying out greetings and what sort of a journey they'd had.

"It's lovely to see you again, such a thrill to be met off the Paris boat-train," Erica was laughing. "Paris was simply marvellous, I can't tell you." She had travelled near the end of the train and talking animatedly, she and Miss Frayle made their way towards the barrier, there was the taxi to find to take them to Liverpool Street, and they circled quickly round groups of people. Hurrying along the front portion of the train, neither of them noticed as they passed the compartment with its gaping doorway blocked by a porter's broad back.

Frozen into immobility for several sickening moments, the porter was staring at the dreadful figure slumped in the corner-seat.

Chapter Seven

AS THE RESULT of a phone call from Superintendent Harper of the Transport Commission Police at Victoria Station, Detective Superintendent "Spider" Bruce of B Division had come over from divisional headquarters at Chelsea, and two men stood bent over a British Railways map spread out on a desk in Superintendent Harper's office. From the open window came the sounds of Victoria Station, the muffled train-announcer's voice, the whistle of arriving and departing trains, together with the rattle of taxis in Hudson Place, with their passengers to and from the Continent.

Action following the porter's discovery in the compartment of the boat-train from Folkestone had been swift and according to routine. The porter had at once sent another porter to fetch the guard while he had remained at the carriage-door. He pulled down the blinds on the platform-side against the possible sight in the compartment being witnessed by any casual passer-by. The guard had promptly dispatched the porter who had fetched him to the office of the Transport Commission Police, and leaving the first porter still where he was he had hurried forthwith to the station-master's office. From there a call was sent to St. George's Hospital at Hyde Park, and within a few minutes an ambulance was on the platform roadway alongside the train.

It had been Superintendent Harper himself who'd come over from his office and gone through the dead man's pockets and produced a passport which gave its owner's name as Johnny Destiny. Comparison with the photograph in the passport and the figure crumpled in the corner didn't amount to much, the dead man's face and head had been dreadfully bashed in. It seemed obvious that he had been looking out of the compartment window and encountered either a passing train or tunnel.

Staring down at the mess it occurred to the railway police-officer that there might be something more to it than a mere accident. For no real reason the idea came to him. Accordingly he hurried back to his office and telephoned Chelsea police-station. He spoke to Detective-Superintendent Bruce.

"May be wasting your invaluable time, I know," he said. "But it looks a bit umpty to me."

"Spider" Bruce said he'd be right over.

Before he left Chelsea, and because the name Johnny Destiny was not entirely unknown to him and also because he knew Superintendent Harper was not the type to get on to him unless he felt there was good reason for doing so, he put a call through to Scotland Yard to enrol the help of the appropriate departments: photographer, fingerprints and all the rest. He also passed the news on to Detective-Inspector Hood.

So it was not until the railway compartment on platform eight at Victoria and its silent, inert passenger in the corner had been given a thorough going-over by the Scotland Yard experts, that the body decorously covered by a blanket was transferred to the waiting ambulance, to be conveyed to the mortuary at St. George's Hospital, where, in accordance with usual practice, it would be duly noted down as dead upon arrival. This made things convenient for the coroner and all concerned, since death having occurred on a moving train, it would be difficult to state exactly in what place, county or district, death had ensued. And the body didn't give a damn anyway.

It was an hour later when the B Division man and Superintendent Harper had got down to considering the map before them. The map was of the railway system between London and Folkestone. Superintendent Harper's bony finger traced the route the train must have taken from Folkestone, then his finger halted.

"Saltwood Tunnel," he said, "near Westenhanger. Nine hundred and fifty-four yards long. That's the first one out of Folkestone." His finger moved along, to pause again. "Sandling Tunnel, about a hundred yards long." His finger moved on. "This one at Sevenoaks, one mile six hundred and ninety-three yards long." Then came Polehill Tunnel, one mile eight hundred and fifty-one miles long. Again the finger shifted, this time to halt on the map at Chelsfield Tunnel, five hundred and ninety-seven yards in its dark length.

Superintendent Harper's finger moved for the last time to a spot between Penge and Sydenham Hill. "This is the Penge Tunnel," he said. "Runs for a mile and three hundred and eighty-one yards, right underneath the Crystal Palace. That's your lot."

Detective-Superintendent Bruce straightened his thick back. "And you say," he said, "that the clearance between the tunnel arch and the train's near-side, that is the left hand side facing the direction it's travelling, is more than enough to allow anyone to lean out of the window without being struck?"

The other scratched his chin. "Of course," he said, "anyone who leans out of a railway-carriage window, except when it's standing at a terminus, and even then only on the platform-side, is asking for it. Why else do we go to such trouble to tell passengers in two or three languages not to? But in fact on this line, anyway, you'd have to lean out a hell of a way to cosh yourself. We did have a case a few week's back of a Peeping Tom who bought it."

"Tell me about that."

"You heard about it, didn't you? Well, there was a honeymoon couple all alone in one compartment and this other chap in the compartment next to it thought he'd be bright and see what they were up to. He was leaning out so far that when the train ran into Polehill Tunnel the archway caught him and didn't do him any good at all. Knocked half his blinking head off."

"They say curiosity kills the cat," Superintendent Bruce said. He thought for a moment. "If it wasn't the tunnel that bashed this chap's head in, it might have been a passing train?"

"On the off-side or right-hand-side? Might be more chance of that. Even though there's plenty of clearance between two passing trains, some of these coaches bulge outwards quite a bit and they rock a bit, too. So a train whipping past another at speed, and a chap's looking out of a window, he might catch a packet. Plenty of trains passing on that line, too. We'll have to wait until we get any reports through from the drivers. Traffic controller at Orpington has been put in the picture. Might come through any minute with some news."

But the B Division man was shaking his head gently.

"I don't think we have to worry about that eventuality," he said. "Blood and mess wasn't on the off-side window." He paused. "I'm very grateful to you, old chap, for sending for me the way you did."

Superintendent Harper gave a deprecating shrug. "I had a hunch there was something that you ought to look into."

"I may be jumping to conclusions," Superintendent Bruce said. But he didn't think he was. He was thinking of Johnny Destiny and all that would go with the sticky end he'd come to.

It was about this time that a burly bowler-hatted figure of over medium height wended his way into Hudson Place at the side of Victoria Station, where Post Office vans, lorries and private cars moved around busily. Past the doorway which led to the royal waiting-room, past the entrance for night-ferry passengers the man padded to turn into a dark green door. On the door: Police London District F Division.

The burly figure removed his bowler-hat to mop his moist forehead with a handkerchief, then replacing his hat he went through another door. He was lighting his pipe as he pushed into Superintendent Harper's office.

"Hello, 'Spider'," he said.

Detective-Superintendent Bruce turned with genial greeting. He indicated his companion. "Superintendent Harper," he said. "Detective-Inspector Hood from Scotland Yard."

Detective-Inspector Hood ambled forward, chewing on his pipe-stem. "This sounds quite interesting," he said. "He had it coming to him. Tell me all you know."

Chapter Eight

MISS FRAYLE HAD to admit to herself that her first impression of Pebcreek was not exactly encouraging. In fact, it looked the last place on earth she would have chosen to spend a holiday. She was sure it was the last place on earth. The end of nowhere. And it was still raining.

The thunderstorm had burst with freakish suddenness. As the Chelmsford train pulled out from Liverpool Street, the sky had been bright blue and with not a cloud to mar its serenity. It wasn't until they reached Shenfield where Miss Frayle and Erica Travers changed for Sharbridge that they realized that it was dark overhead and threatening, the atmosphere full of foreboding.

"It's going to rain," Miss Frayle said mildly, as they waited for their train to arrive.

"You can say that again," Erica said. "In for a monsoon by the look of it." She muttered bitterly to the effect that it would definitely never happen in Paris. The French had this sort of thing so much more under control.

As their train rattled out of Shenfield for Sharbridge, the first fork of lightning split the swollen sky with a searing flash and the thunder crashed directly overhead. Erica groaned with vexation and Miss Frayle stared morosely at the shadowed landscape and then the carriage window was a blurred rectangle as the rain buffetted it, completely cutting off any view. Erica groaned out aloud. "Isn't this absolutely unspeakable," she said, her pretty mouth a rebellious line, eyes flashing with frustration.

Miss Frayle was forced to agree that it didn't look too good, and her face became fixed in a disconsolate expression.

The storm had moved inland by the time the train drew into Sharbridge station, some three-quarters of an hour later, but as Miss Frayle and Erica got out of the station to the bus that was to convey them on the last stage of their journey it was still raining hard, the sky was still overcast.

The uncomfortable journey in the rattling bus had heightened her growing disillusionment, had brought pangs of regret that she had accepted Erica's invitation to share a holiday in this desolate corner of the Essex marshes.

It would be so different, Erica had said. Peering through the rain-splashed bus-window Miss Frayle decided that the only difference was, no matter how far they travelled, the scene outside remained the same. From Sharbridge to Pebcreek the world was flat and grey, criss-crossed with creeks and dykes, marshland and river walls, with only here and there a boarded cottage or spinney to break the monotony.

The drab scene outside emphasized by the weather seemed to effect the steamy atmosphere inside the half-empty bus, for Erica had subsided into silence, hardly saying a word throughout the twenty-five-minute journey.

At last the bus stopped outside a weather-boarded cottage which identified itself as Pebcreek post office. Erica brightened a little.

"Here we are," she said, and with the conductor lending a hand with their three suitcases she and Miss Frayle got off the bus into the rain, carrying a suitcase in one hand, and the third between them. They crossed the narrow street to shelter in the porch of the Safe Harbour.

"Of course, it's all quite different when the sun's shining," Erica had said with an attempt at a smile. "I couldn't have picked a worse day to introduce you."

Miss Frayle had slipped off her horn-rimmed glasses and was drying them with a handkerchief.

"You can't help the weather," Miss Frayle said. She tried to infuse a cheerful note into her voice; but with her wet stockings clinging coldly to her legs and the awful shriek of the swinging inn-sign above setting her teeth on edge, it was not easy to sound happy. She tried to rouse some interest in her new surroundings, but what she could see through the rain did not contribute to a holiday feeling either.

Pebcreek seemed to consist of one street in which the most prominent building appeared to be the old inn, under whose porch they were now sheltering. The porch itself gave the impression of being likely to collapse in the not too distant future, Miss Frayle thought. Where it had been bolted to the door posts the wood was breaking away, the salt air had loosened some of the bolts so that there was a gap between the porch and the building where rain trickled through, while the structure leaned slightly towards the road conveying the impression of a departing customer who had imbibed too freely.

The red single-decker bus, giving a certain touch of colour to the scene, turned round and went back the way it had come. Miss Frayle noticed that the boarded cottage proclaiming itself the post office, in front of which the bus had stood, seemed to be the only inviting place she could see. Cream-painted it had a large bowl of flowers displayed in the parlour window next to the shop door.

Next to the post office along the street ran a terrace of slate-roofed cottages with the same weather-boarded walls. They were small and quaint with wooden palings fringing each tiny square garden, and although the paintwork was weathered, the windows were neatly curtained. There appeared to be no signs of life in them.

At the end of this row stood a double-fronted shop with Pebcreek Stores over the windows, in which was displayed a miscellany of goods from a length of smoked bacon to a box of washing powder. Miss Frayle could make out a couple of people in the shop.

The one brick building was at the end of the street, a small house designed in modern style, a blue plaque at the side of the door announcing it to be the police station. It occurred to Miss Frayle that with only a further half-a-dozen houses and a barn-like building neighbouring the inn, making up the sum total of Pebcreek, there seemed to be little for a policeman to do.

Beyond the houses opposite she caught a glimpse of the river. Greyish-brown it looked as cold and uninviting as the Thames at Blackfriars. She could just see the river wall on the further side. But the curtain of rain cut off the rest of the picture, though she imagined the scene to continue without change, just as it had appeared from the bus.

The Safe Harbour stood on the village fringe, and just to their right the street narrowed to become little more than a side road following the river. Here two or three tarred and dilapidated sheds jutted out over the mud. On one shed Miss Frayle could just discern the faded words: BOAT BUILDER. The road ran on parallel with the river, sometimes below the river wall and sometimes level with it, strange and lonely.

With a little shiver Miss Frayle turned her attention to Erica, sitting on her suitcase nonchalantly replacing the make-up the rain had washed off her face. Miss Frayle recalled Erica mentioning in the train that they would be met at Pebcreek with a car. There was no sign of a car at all; but Miss Frayle concluded that Erica obviously had hopes of it arriving and soon, else why should she bother with her appearance?

Miss Frayle, leaning against the side of the porch, smiled in spite of her discomfort. "Didn't you say someone was going to be here to meet us?"

Erica put the mirror and lipstick back into her bag. "That wretched Jim Rayner," she said. "Swore on his sacred oath he'd be here at the bus-stop. He's probably tinkering with his blessed car." She sighed with annoyance. "Wouldn't mind so much if it wasn't raining. Isn't very far to walk, there's a short cut to the creek."

"Does he live on a boat, too?" Miss Frayle said.

Erica shook her head. "Got a cottage not far from the *Moya*. Lives there all the summer and spends his winters in Chelsea. Just like him not to appear when he's wanted most. An artist, and not too reliable. Can't say I'm surprised at this, but I didn't expect we'd run into the North Sea as well." And she stared out irritably at the driving rain.

"No chance of a taxi, or anything?" Miss Frayle said.

"Nothing like that here. Everyone goes by boat."

"Oh," Miss Frayle said uncertainly. "We'll just have to wait and hope. There seems to be a break coming in the clouds over there." She infused all the optimism of which she was capable into her tone, and indicated the northwest, where a vein of light streaked the dark-grey cloud-mass. "If it eases off we could start walking."

"Terribly sorry it's such a ghastly start for you," Erica said. "But honest, once you're on board and the weather clears, you'll lap up every moment."

Miss Frayle smiled at her and they both stood watching and waiting for the skies to lift or a car to show up. But despite the lightening sky, the rain continued to imprison them in the inn porch for another quarter-hour. Then as suddenly as it had begun it slackened and in a miraculously few moments a watery sun cheered their surroundings. The rain became a few isolated drops and Erica and Miss Frayle took advantage of the break and started quickly down the river road.

"Might have to take shelter again," Erica said with a glance at the sky. "But at least we'll be half-way there."

"How far is Dormouse Creek?" Miss Frayle said.

"Two miles by river, one and a half by road; under a mile by this short cut." Erica pointed ahead. "See that little copse in front?"

Miss Frayle looked beyond the curl of the road to where it climbed a gentle rise. At the top was a shallow stone wall, trees and shrubs grew in a neglected cluster behind it. Some of the trees looked dead and among them she could detect the grey stonework of a crumbling building.

"We turn off on a footpath just the other side of it," Erica was saying.

Miss Frayle said: "What's that building among the trees? A ruin of some kind?"

"Pebcreek Church, or what's left of it," Erica said. "Ages back Pebcreek used to be on the low-lying ground next to the river. But the place was flooded, practically washed away in a great storm. Most of the people drowned. Those who were left built a new village on higher ground, above the river, as you saw. This old church was never used, and it's gradually caved in."

Miss Frayle recollected having noticed a church, as they came into the village on the bus. She remembered it looked comparatively new. Seventy or eighty years old. Her attention riveted on the spot where the old village had been. There was a grass wall and a steep dyke separating the site from the river now, but the ground appeared marshy and treacherous, criss-crossed with sedge-lined drains. Nothing grew there except spiky tufts of grass and clusters of short, tiny-headed mauve flowers. They made a pretty carpet of colour in their drab surroundings, the sun had gone in and the sky looked threatening again. A low distant rumble of thunder rolled across the wide open country, and Miss Frayle quickened her pace.

"Another shower," Erica said grimly. "Better make for the shelter of the trees."

"Trees in a thunderstorm?" Miss Frayle said anxiously.

"Oh. Then we can shelter in the ruins."

As they climbed the rise Miss Frayle saw the full width of the river. She was surprised to find so much water. It had given the impression of being narrow when she had seen it at the village. She thought the tide was coming in and decided that could account for the fact that it appeared so much broader.

The few feet they climbed above the river-level gave her a view of a strange waste that was neither land or water. In the distance she could see the sea, and between that and where they stood spread a great area of marsh fissured by tidal creeks and dyke-walls, with the river itself a broad winding ribbon between them. Closer to them the scene was broken by tiny islets on which stunted trees had taken grip.

The rain suddenly came in sharp spatters, blown out of the sky on the wings of a fierce squall that shook the branches of the trees. Erica quickly led the way through a clump of gorse and a gap in the stone wall towards a ruined archway that had once been the porch of the old church. The place was overgrown with elder shrubs and nettles. It was not until Miss Frayle stumbled over a shallow mound and fell against a sharp weathered stone that she realized she was in a graveyard.

Miss Frayle had considered the ruin an isolated monument; she had not given a thought to the likelihood of it having a burial ground, which the trees and wild vegetation had concealed. Somewhat overcome by the eeriness of the place she hung back.

The wind moaned through the trees, and showers of rain scattered down from their branches and spattered her. Now she could make out a host of moss-sprinkled tombstones all round her, it was as if, she thought fearfully, they had suddenly risen up out of the weed-infested tangle against her intrusion. She was reminded of a very similar occasion one evening last summer when she had accompanied Dr. Morelle down to an old church on the river.

She'd found herself in the darkness stumbling over old graves in pursuit of Dr. Morelle who had been bent only upon finding the particular grave-stone he had come in search of. She hadn't enjoyed that macabre experience very much. This was almost as unnerving; though it wasn't night. The atmosphere of the dark, thunderous early evening was decidedly sinister.

Another peal of thunder rolled far off across the marshes, and she knew she must get out from under the trees. She looked to where Erica, who had grabbed both her own suitcases to lighten Miss Frayle's load, had pushed on to the old stone porch and was beckoning her.

"Come on, what's holding you up?"

"I fell over somebody's grave," Miss Frayle said, apologetically and scrambling breathlessly to the other's side.

"Place is full of old graves," Erica said, "but no one's been buried here for donkey's years."

Miss Frayle found herself marvelling at Erica's cool indifference to her surroundings, she was staring through the trees to the sky above the marsh. "I don't think we're going to get this lot," she said confidently. "It's rolling away over Burnham. We've only got the tail-end."

"Hope so," Miss Frayle said. "The sooner we're out of this creepy place the better." She threw a look at the old porch and a broken ivy-covered wall. Some of the lattices still gaped in the crumbling walls, one of which ended in all that remained of the vestry. This had a steep sloping roof from which most of the slate had gone, covered in creeper. Nettles grew high around it screening a short arched door. The gaps in the stonework under what had once been the gable formed a colony of nests. Birds flew to and fro.

"The sun's shining again," Erica was saying, "over there."

Miss Frayle peered through the trees across the deserted road to the river.

"Someone's in a boat," she said. She watched a small, open motorboat move slowly against the tide with two oilskin-clad figures in her.

"Fishing by the look of it," Erica said. Then suddenly she was listening, her eyes on the road. "There's a car coming from Dormouse Creek direction. It could be Jim. Hear it? Sounds as if it's on its last legs, that'll be him."

Quickly Erica picked up one case and plunged through the graveyard towards the road, intent on stopping the approaching car before it had rattled past.

Miss Frayle was about to follow when a sudden flutter of wings brought her attention round to the ruined vestry. The birds flew off into the trees, chattering in alarm. Miss Frayle thought Erica's sudden dash towards the approaching car must have disturbed them. Then she realized with a shock that it wasn't that at all. She stood staring, too scared to move.

The door under the creeper-covered vestry roof was slowly opening.

Chapter Nine

MISS FRAYLE STOOD still, the sound of her heart loud in her ears. Momentarily she had forgotten that Erica Travers was only a few yards away, standing in the road frantically waving at the oncoming sports-car. Miss Frayle had eyes only for the moving door.

A figure of a man appeared. Too far away and partly screened by shrubs and creeper for her to see him clearly, Miss Frayle saw only the back of his long raincoat. A dark hat covered his head. He half-turned towards the road, attracted by Erica's voice and the sound of the car engine. Then he pushed the door to, and stumbled off with a limp, disappearing into the shadows of the trees beyond.

Erica was calling to her, and Miss Frayle blinking behind her horn-rims, pulled herself together and forced her legs to carry her through the graveyard to the road.

When she joined Erica she showed no signs of the agitation she had suffered. She managed to smile brightly to the young man Erica was introducing.

"Jim Rayner," Erica said. "Whose family motto is: 'Better late than never'."

Jim Rayner grinned ruefully. He was a sun-tanned young man with tousled reddish hair. His eyes were greenish with a friendly glint in them and Miss Frayle judged that despite her joking tone, Erica was obviously delighted to see him. "Look at us," Erica was saying. "Wet, tired and our stockings so laddered they're only good for firemen."

"I'm darned sorry, Erica," Jim said. "But I just couldn't get the so-and-so to start."

He indicated the ancient-looking touring car behind him, which it seemed to Miss Frayle, should have gone to the scrap-heap twenty years ago. There were rents in the canvas hood and no sidescreens. The seats were low on the floor. There was only one windscreen wiper and the body and wings were dented. It was painted green, but it was difficult to see the colour through the mud. The nicest parts about it were the headlamps, Miss Frayle thought. They were huge, round and chromium.

"Mag trouble," Jim Rayner said. "She got a soaking last night, and I had to bake it." He noticed Miss Frayle looking at the car, and added proudly: "She's real vintage, you know. Don't make anything like them to-day."

"Can you blame them," Erica said quickly. "But will it go now?"

Miss Frayle noticed that the engine had stopped.

"Get in and we'll run her down the hill."

Erica climbed into the back wedged in with the suitcases, while Miss Frayle sat in front. When she had finally arranged her legs under the dashboard, Jim Rayner dropped himself next to her into the driving seat, switched on, pushed the short gear lever into first gear and kept his foot on the clutch, then released the handbrake. The car started to coast down the incline, just as it began raining again.

"Once she's away, I'll turn round in that gateway there," Jim said.

Without any warning he suddenly let in the clutch. The car jolted almost to a stop and Miss Frayle was thrown forward and just managed to save herself hitting the windscreen. The engine misfired and roared and the car lurched forward again and Miss Frayle was forced back hard in the seat. While Miss Frayle rearranged her skirt and straightened her glasses, the young man beside her said agreeably:

"You all right, Miss Frayle?"

"I'm all right," Miss Frayle said, and prepared herself for the next shock. But Jim was careful after that. He turned round smoothly in the gateway and drove sedately up the hill and passed the copse again.

Miss Frayle could see little of where she was going in spite of being in the front. Rain splashed the cracked windscreen so that her vision was blurred beyond the bonnet and if she turned to look out of the side she had the rain in her face as well as all the drops that blew in from the side of the hood. She pressed herself as far into the centre of the car as she could, and told Erica over her shoulder about the man appearing out of the vestry.

"They say the place is supposed to be haunted," Jim said when she had finished. Miss Frayle glanced at him, and he grinned at her cheerfully.

"Nonsense," Erica said quickly. "That's an old story that got around years ago. Probably a tramp you saw, sheltering from the rain. Same as us."

The subject was forgotten as the road turned away from the river, suddenly climbed over a steep wooded rise, and Jim changed down with a crashing of gears. Slowing almost to a walking pace he negotiated a sharp hump-backed bridge with the remark that he didn't want Miss Frayle's head to make a hole in his hood. He drove on slowly.

The rain had slackened and Miss Frayle, sensing that they were nearing their destination at last, glanced out of the car.

She could see a stretch of meadowland with stunted trees lining a wide ditch. On the further side a small herd of black and white cattle grazed, beyond was a river wall and she guessed Dormouse Creek lay behind this. The grassy wall continued endlessly towards where she imagined the main river to be. But she was as yet too low to see the creek.

A little further along the road broadened and levelled itself with the wall which had now become a kind of wooden quay. There were mooring-rings attached to the timbers and a broken-down flagstaff. A small jetty stuck out into the water and there was a clumsy-looking rowing-boat tied up to the jetty ladder. Thirty or forty yards away from the quay, just below where the river wall began was a rambling two-storey brick and boarded building which Jim Rayner pointed to.

As they slowly passed Miss Frayle could see the sign and for a moment a vision passed across her mind of someone swinging from a gallows. The inexplicable mental picture vanished and with a shiver she saw that it was an inn-sign, picturing the faded figure of a man carrying a gun, with a dog at his heels, above it the inscription: *The Wildfowler*. It looked a drab, depressing place, but she had to confess to herself that the weather and the desolate scene accounted for the impression she received.

"Dormouse Creek?" Miss Frayle said to Erica indicating the mud and water. "Where's the houseboat?"

"If this rattletrap had a wiper you'd see it from here," Erica said.

"There's our store." Jim was pointing to a cottage with a neat hedge lining the road, old advertisements for tea and pickles plastered on the windows of its single front room. "Paraffin for your oil-lamps, and new-laid eggs for breakfast."

"Are there any other houseboats besides the *Moya*?" Miss Frayle said.

"Two more," Erica leaned forward. "But they're all moored a good distance from each other, so no one's really overlooked."

"Best of this spot, you know," Jim said. "The scenery might be flat and unspectacular, facilities practically *nil*, but you can do just as you like without fear of being taken for a crank. Even weekends during the height of the summer, it never gets crowded. Apart from the odd yacht ditch-crawling, you hardly see a stranger from one week's end to another. Yet Southend isn't fifteen miles away."

Then Jim Rayner was stopping the car beside a long black hull moored to the bank a few yards away.

"Here we are," Erica said. Miss Frayle caught the excitement in her voice, and the next moment she was out of the car.

Jim got out and dragged the suitcases after him, placing them on the grassy bank at the end of a narrow gangway leading to the deck of the houseboat. The rain had practically stopped, but the wind was still strong, jostling the low clouds impatiently above the landscape. An invigorating and salty tang filled the air, mixed with it the boaty smell of tar and rope, and the peculiar scent of the marsh.

The only sign of life aboard the *Moya* was a wisp of smoke that was whisked away from the bent chimney. The boat must have been seventy feet in length, heavily-built in a way that reminded Miss Frayle of those old sailing-barges she had seen on the Thames. It had a stumpy mast and wide, clean decks with a long varnished coach roof containing two pairs of skylights. The large round portholes in the coaming were fringed with curtains and there was a big sliding-hatch leading below.

The coach roof ended aft in a deckhouse with large observation windows on all sides and this opened on to a wide afterdeck with a space enough for deck-chairs when the sun was shining. Although the hull was black and it sat on the mud over which the tide was now creeping, Miss Frayle thought it looked most attractive, with its bright metal work and varnished superstructure.

"See you this evening," Jim said to Miss Frayle as he climbed into the car. He had dumped the suitcases on the deck.

"I've asked him over for a drink," Erica said.

"Where do you live?" Miss Frayle said as she and Erica watched from the end of the gangway, wondering if he would get his engine to start. He pointed over a bramble-covered bank where a white cottage stood among the trees.

"I hope Erica will bring you over," he said, and pressed the starter. After a couple of attempts the engine roared into life and the car jerked off in a stream of blue exhaust smoke. They watched him head in the direction of his cottage.

"He's nice, even if slightly mad," Erica as she turned on the gangway. "Come on." She led the way up to the deck and went aft. "We'll find Aunt Edith below. I'll take you down through the deckhouse, the companion's not so awkward as the hatch."

Erica opened the door and went in. As Miss Frayle turned to follow, her attention was attracted along the road towards the Wildfowler Inn. It was deserted save for one figure. A man in a long raincoat and dark hat.

Chapter Ten

FOR A MOMENT Miss Frayle could have sworn it was the man she had seen in the ruins of the graveyard, but as the figure approached she decided she must be mistaken. On such a day and in this part of the world, she could, she felt, expect to see several people similarly dressed. Besides, she saw now, with an involuntary relaxation of the tension which had once more so oddly seized her, that this man did not walk with a limp.

She heard Erica call and with a little smile at her foolish fears she went into the deckhouse. The novel and comfortable surroundings in which she found herself immediately drove any alarming thoughts that may have troubled her completely from her mind.

Aunt Edith made a surprising and undeniably impressive impact, her individual appearance and personality was unique in Miss Frayle's experience, and during her employment with Dr. Morelle she had encountered not a few extraordinary types.

Erica's aunt was a tall, hefty-looking woman in her early fifties. She wore dark blue sailcloth trousers hitched round her ample waist with a leather belt, and the thick navy jersey. Her hair was dark, close-cropped with hardly a streak of grey, and with her strong sunburnt face and neck gave her a somewhat fierce appearance, no doubt capable of taking command of any situation, but there were laughter-lines around her blue eyes, and a twinkle in them.

She reminded Miss Frayle irresistibly of a good-natured pirate.

Miss Frayle had first been taken aback by the other's appearance when she had barged through the further door as Erica and herself had stepped off the companion-ladder from the deckhouse into the large comfortably furnished cabin which Erica described as the saloon.

"Aunt Edith, this is Miss Frayle," Erica said and the big woman came forward an arm outstretched. "Miss Travers."

"How do you do, Miss Travers —"

"Call me Aunt Edith, it'll be easier." And then the other went on to explain that she had heard their arrival, but couldn't show herself as she was just changing her trousers. Miss Frayle had winced a trifle under the

55

pressure of the handshake and had been surprised once more at the toughness of the woman's skin. It was hard and calloused, as if she had been pulling ropes or rowing a boat all her life.

"Some fool in the village," Aunt Edith was saying, "said they'd seen a black-necked grebe up at Willow Mere. I was sure it was a mistake, but had to go up to see. All I found was a curlew. I was pretty wet I can tell you. I didn't mind that but on the way back stepped into a mudhole. I was cleaning up when I heard the car." She smiled at them. "Just as well you were late. I suppose young Rayner's box-of-tricks broke down?"

"It wouldn't start," Erica said. "We walked as far as the old church and he caught up with us there."

"About where he'll end up if he drives that old wreck much longer," Aunt Edith said. "In the churchyard. Still, I'm glad he turned up. I expect you're hungry and damp. I lit the fire because I knew you'd want to dry out. Take Miss Frayle and show her to her quarters, and the bathroom."

Miss Frayle followed Erica across the saloon and out through the door by which Aunt Edith had appeared. She found herself in a bright cream-painted corridor with a low-beamed ceiling. Erica explained that they were now going for'ard and that the narrow doors on their right with polished brass handles were the cabins. The first door was Aunt Edith's, next the bathroom, then came the midship companion leading down from the sliding hatch Miss Frayle had noticed from outside. Next were the guest's cabins. Three in all, and two of them double-berthed. Erica had the first, and Miss Frayle the one next door.

"Where does that door lead?" Miss Frayle said, pointing to the handle in the bulkhead at the end of the corridor.

"Fo'c'sle," Erica said. "It's got four folding berths. Right up for'ard is the store for everything. Paint, ropes, paraffin. Aunt's got everything imaginable in there. You get to it through the hatch in the foredeck." She opened the door of the cabin.

Miss Frayle stepped over the high threshold into a small bedroom, with a low berth on each side. Between the foot of each bunk at the end of the cabin was a neat dressing-table. On either side of this filling the space under the side-deck was a wardrobe. Under the berths were long drawers and the floor was covered with plain blue carpet. In the corner behind the door was a tall enamel jug and above it a folding washbasin.

"I'm afraid there's no water laid on, except in Aunt Edith's cabin," Erica said. "Have to get your water from the bathroom."

"It's wonderful," Miss Frayle said. She was impressed by the comfort she had certainly not expected to find when she had seen the boat from outside. "Where does the water for the bathroom come from?"

"Big covered tank on the fo'c'sle," Erica said. "It's for'ard of the mast, I don't suppose you noticed it. Pipes run from it to the bathroom, Aunt's cabin and the galley."

"Who fills the tank?"

"The shop we passed. Got a pump in the back garden. Clear spring water. When our supply gets low, the chap comes over with his water-trolley and pumps us a tank full."

Miss Frayle looked around, the cabin seemed so spacious; everything was painted cream and as well as the large porthole, there was an opening skylight of opaque glass above.

"What do you think of her?" Erica said. "Aunt Edith? I told you she was quite a character."

"She's very nice," Miss Frayle said. "Different from anyone, I've ever met. She's mad about wild birds, isn't she?"

"Her one interest in life. That and this boat." She smiled at Miss Frayle, as if thankful that the meeting between her and Aunt Edith had gone off so well. "I'll leave you to get sorted out." Erica moved to the door. "I'm sure we're going to have a wonderful time."

"I'm sure," Miss Frayle said.

"That old sun will do its stuff to-morrow, don't you fret," Erica went on. "We can go down the creek in the dinghy. There's a nice sandy strip, fine for swimming when the tide's up. Or you can just loaf about in your swimsuit."

"What ought I to wear this evening, Erica?"

"Slacks, of course," Erica said promptly. "I'm going to. And a shirt, or sweater, if you think you'll be cold."

Miss Frayle's eyelashes fluttered behind the lens of her glasses.

"Mr. Rayner will be coming in for a drink, you said. I was going to put on a dress."

"Jim," Erica said, "you won't need to worry about him. He'll turn up in the first thing he can lay his hands on. Sou-wester and thigh-boots, or running shorts and bare feet. If he turns up at all, probably forget and be tinkering with that car of his."

When Miss Frayle made her way back to the saloon-cabin the table was laid for supper. She could hear Miss Travers, or Aunt Edith as she automatically thought of her, singing to herself in the galley, and she guessed that Erica had not yet finished changing. She stood there, contemplating her unusual surroundings, and rather conscious of her dark blue slacks, which together with her swimsuit, she had bought especially for this holiday, and the white turtle-neck sweater she wore.

The cream-painted walls of the saloon was sectioned into panels by thin varnished battens. There were three portholes on either side of the coach roof and a skylight over the centre. Framed photographs of birds were everywhere and several water-colours of marshland scenes. One showed a skein of geese above an estuary, another depicted a small yacht anchored in some lonely creek with a great expanse of marsh and sky its background.

A ship's clock ticked away on the bulkhead near the sliding-door which opened past the galley to the companion up to the deckhouse. In spite of it being open, the cabin was warm. There were two easy chairs either side the sliding door. There was a sideboard and a drink cabinet which together with a small writing-desk and dining chairs, made up the saloon-cabin's furniture.

Miss Frayle moved hesitantly to the doorway and looked into the galley. Aunt Edith turned from the stove. "Come in and see my kitchen," she said.

Miss Frayle stepped into the roomy recess, staring about her with admiration. The modern sink with draining boards flanking it under the porthole. White-painted cupboards and shelves fixed along one side. A large paraffin-stove with an oven and on the asbestos shelf next to it, a pressure-stove with the kettle steaming on it. Above were wide shelves and hooks holding a variety of kitchenware.

"You cook by oil?" Miss Frayle said chattily.

"Safest in a boat," Aunt Edith said, dexterously transferring the kettle of water to the teapot. "It's tea with every meal here," she said. "As well as between meals. No, if you use gas and there happens to be a leak it's liable to seep into your bilges. Then one day — woof! I shouldn't like to lose the *Moya*. I've spent a long time shaping the old tub to my tastes."

"It's certainly a wonderful boat," Miss Frayle said. "My cabin's lovely."

"It's comfortable. Don't mind roughing it outside, but I like my creature comforts when I come back home."

"Erica told me you were an ornithologist," Miss Frayle said.

"Nuts about wild birds is the way she put it, I'll bet. And she couldn't be more right. Autumn's one of the best times, of course. But the summer's interesting, too."

"It must be a bit lonely in the winter," Miss Frayle said.

"You're never lonely when you've plenty to do. And the folk around here may be few and far between, but they're good company when you get to know them, and they get to know you. Took them a long time to accept me."

After supper of ham and eggs, Miss Frayle insisted on helping Erica wash up while Aunt Edith lit up a cheroot and made copious notes about her afternoon excursion in a leather-bound exercise book. Erica then took Miss Frayle on a further inspection of the *Moya*, while at the same time adding to her description of her holiday in Paris which she had omitted during the journey down from Liverpool Street.

It was about half-past eight when they sat in the deckhouse and Aunt Edith appeared with a tray of drinks. Gin, rum, whisky and a decanter of red wine. Miss Frayle settled for a glass of wine, Erica a little gin; and Aunt Edith took a glass of rum and returned to her notes. Presently Erica went off to the galley to iron out some creases in her tapering slacks. Miss Frayle went out on deck.

The rain had completely stopped, the clouds dispersed, the oncoming night was still. The sky was like shot-silk in the west where the sun sunk beneath a few last ragged banners of cloud. The tide was slowly filling the creek, gently lifting the *Moya* off the soft mud. The dinghy was floating astern, its painter outstretched, and the flood stream made the faintest whisper as it trickled past its planks.

Miss Frayle's gaze wandered up the creek. There were the two other houseboats Erica had mentioned, each some distance away from each other. A yacht rode midstream, and a couple of sailing dinghies were moored to the bank, just about opposite Jim Rayner's cottage. Further along, past the little white house between the trees, she could see the white tops of two trailer caravans. Beyond them was a farm, and between the farm and the creek were two pairs of cottages. These and the inn and the shop, it seemed, added up to Dormouse Creek.

Miss Frayle turned to look down the creek again, lost in the strange fascination of the great marsh. Here and there a light twinkled, a boat on the distant river perhaps or a lonely farmhouse. A blue haze began to form on the horizon and turned slowly to a white mist out of which rose the plaintive cries of wildfowl.

Miss Frayle was startled by a voice suddenly in her ear.

"Fallen under its spell, eh?" She turned to find Jim Rayner at her side. "Knew you would, anyone with a spark of romance in them is sold on the place the first night."

"I didn't hear you," Miss Frayle said.

"Sorry if I made you jump. It's these shoes." He was Wearing old canvas shoes, once white, but now a dirty-grey. Miss Frayle crossed to the deckhouse. She found his sudden appearance against the stillness which seemed to vibrate the air about her almost overpowering. "Erica and Aunt Edith are below," she said uncertainly. "Perhaps we'd better go down."

She reached the companion and then felt his hand on her arm. She gave a nervous little gasp. But he was only grinning at her.

"On boats a man precedes a girl," he said. "Just in case you slip. I mean it would be a worse fate for you to break your neck than for me to break your fall. Or wouldn't it?"

He went down the companion and waited for her at the bottom. Miss Frayle found herself blushing a little as he looked up at her. "Okay," he said. "Let yourself go."

Chapter Eleven

IT WAS A little while before Miss Frayle could sleep.

She lay there in her comfortable berth, listening to the sounds that crept in through the open porthole. The gentle lap of water, a strange spongy sound, as if the mudbanks were breathing again as the receding tide exposed them to the moonlit air; the intermittent calls of the wildfowl, the faint hoot of an owl in nearby trees. Mingled with them all the pungent scent of the marsh.

But what kept sleep from her was the insistent picture on her mind of the limping man in the old churchyard. Despite the excitement of getting acquainted with the boat and Aunt Edith, the memory of the incident which had seemed to her at the time odd and macabre, had not been dispelled. She tried to recall it with a calm detachment. She had no doubt that Erica was right; and yet had the man been no more than some tramp, sheltering from the storm?

Miss Frayle made a resolute effort to shift her thoughts. Aunt Edith had been wonderful company, talking racily over her rum and cheroot about the experiences she'd met on her bird-watching expeditions. Jim Rayner, too, had provided quite considerable amusement recounting some of his adventures in sailing dinghies and motor-boats. The evening had passed so quickly, Miss Frayle had been surprised to find it was midnight when she had gone to her cabin.

It was Jim Rayner who had come up with the idea of going over to Southend in his ancient car to-morrow. He had suggested the trip to Erica on the spur of the moment, as he was leaving. He was going to Southend, he explained, to see the publicity people at the Kursaal about a poster he was doing for them. Why didn't Erica and Miss Frayle come along with him?

Miss Frayle admitted she'd never been to Southend, and he had at once assured her it was an opportunity that shouldn't be passed up lightly. Aunt Edith had agreed that to experience the delights of the pier and the Kursaal was something not to be missed, or the reverse, according to whichever way you looked at it. Then Erica had thought it might be fun. So it was fixed.

Privately, Miss Frayle felt she would much preferred to have explored the locality of Dormouse Creek; but after all, there was the remainder of her stay in which to do that. Jim Rayner arranged to pick them up at half-past nine in the morning, but the arrangement depended on the weather. No point in leaving the snug comfort of the houseboat for a chilly journey to Southend in that excuse for a car, Erica said.

Miss Frayle turned and glanced out of the porthole at the circle of summer night-sky. Calm and full of promise for the coming day, it seemed. With a guilty start she suddenly realized that she hadn't given a thought to Dr. Morelle, so full had been her mind of her arrival on on board the *Moya*. She wondered, and now she began to feel more sleepy, how he had managed. He had flatly refused to engage a temporary secretary in her absence, but she had arranged on his behalf for an agency to cope with any recordings of dictation, and to supply a stenographer to deal with his mail, whenever he required it.

Of course, Miss Frayle had planned the holiday carefully so that it would coincide with a relatively inactive stretch in Dr. Morelle's work. She just hoped nothing arose which might justify Dr. Morelle recalling her from her holiday back to Harley Street. She wouldn't put it past him, if he really worked himself into the mood.

She began wishing he would plan his life so that he, too, could take a holiday. But he scorned such an idea, and she felt that in a way he was right. She could not picture him relaxing in a deck-chair, or lounging about sun-bathing. At last she fell asleep with a smile of faint amusement at the idea of Dr. Morelle behaving like any ordinary man.

Miss Frayle dreamed not about life aboard the *Moya*; or about the trip to Southend Pier. What she did dream of was an overcast sky, ominous and sinister, and that she was on her way along a road across the marshes to some destination of which she was uncertain. Some of the time her footsteps dragged, at others she found herself running; and all the time she could not seem to pass the ruined church amidst half-buried gravestones and crumbling vestry. And a dark figure kept appearing and disappearing in and out of the shadowy trees in the churchyard, limping. Only it wasn't the man in the long raincoat and hat, it was Dr. Morelle.

Miss Frayle awoke to a morning that fulfilled the promise of the night before. The wind was gentle and from the east and the sun beat down from a cloudless sky. Soon the decks of the *Moya* were so warm the heat crept through the soles of Miss Frayle's shoes.

She and Erica wore light summer frocks, Erica the one she had bought in Paris. A few minutes after nine-thirty they heard a report like the firing of a double-barrelled gun.

"That'll be it," Erica said to Miss Frayle.

A minute or two later, Jim Rayner came into their view in the rattletrap car and they watched it as it chugged up the road and swept alongside the *Moya* in flamboyant style.

Jim Rayner was in an exuberant mood, his rusty hair as tousled as ever, his sunburnt features cracked with a grin. Erica squeezed into the back of the car, Jim warning her to mind the portfolio of drawings that he had thrown there. Miss Frayle climbed in beside him, he let in the clutch carefully and they moved off. As they roared away Aunt Edith appeared, to wave the paraffin-can in farewell.

The drive to Southend was pleasant, much of the way the landscape reminded Miss Frayle of that around Dormouse Creek. Gradually the pattern changed. The dykes and streams and little bridges gave way to farmland. The villages were larger; the country became gently undulating in places and there were more trees.

The car rattled and coughed through the small town of Crayford, and a little later was joining heavier traffic on the outskirts of Westcliff and Southend.

Presently Jim pulled up in a side street off the main thoroughfare.

"We made it," he said, reaching into the back for his portfolio. "All in one piece." Miss Frayle got out and Erica followed. "Look, I don't expect to be more than about twenty minutes. There's a coffee-bar round the corner. Why don't you nip in there and I'll join you? I'll be twenty minutes at the most."

Erica and Miss Frayle found a vacant table in the corner of the coffee-bar and their coffee had only just arrived when Jim suddenly appeared, minus his portfolio and his smile.

"Damned bore," he said, "but I've got to go into a bit of a conference about the job. Alterations and that, so God knows what time I'll be free. Terribly sorry, but you'll have to show yourselves around."

"I expect we'll manage," Erica said. "Where and when do we meet up with you?"

"It'll be after lunch," Jim said. "We'd better meet here, say at three." He pulled a wry face. "Can't even stop for a coffee." He turned away. "Be good and don't speak to any strange men."

As he went out the man at the table next to Miss Frayle and Erica also got up to leave. He brushed a newspaper off the table-corner; what attracted Erica's attention to it as it fell to the floor was a headline on the front page, MAN FOUND DEAD ON BOAT TRAIN.

The man didn't pick it up as he left the shop. Erica grabbed it with wide eyes. It was a London morning paper. Her gaze fastened on the picture in the column next to the story. She gave an exclamation.

"It's the man I met on the boat."

"Who?" Miss Frayle said. She had observed Erica's interest in the newspaper with some curiosity.

Erica pointed to the photograph. "He's been found dead in the train at Victoria with his head bashed in."

"Oh?" Miss Frayle took the paper and read the story. "Johnny Destiny," she said slowly. "Was that his name?"

Erica gave a shrug. "He didn't tell me his name. But it's him all right."

"It says my friend Inspector Hood is on the case," Miss Frayle said.

"Your friend?" Erica flashed her a quick look.

"He and Dr. Morelle are great pals," Miss Frayle said. "He's a dear, I'm very fond of Inspector Hood."

Erica was eyeing her with an expression of mingled envy and respect which Miss Frayle could not help finding somewhat gratifying. Then she saw the other frown to herself and stir her coffee thoughtfully. She did not attempt to drink it.

"What is it?" she said.

"I told you I met him."

"I know," Miss Frayle said, blinking anxiously behind her glasses. "I'm sorry if it's upset you —"

Erica interrupted her with a sudden shake of her head. "It wasn't only that," she said. "There was another man. A man who seemed to be watching him. He was there in the background. I told him about it," she indicated the photograph. "But he just laughed it off. Said it was probably another American —" She broke off. "Oh, I expect I'm imagining things, only it didn't seem like that to me. It was as if this man watching him knew him."

"And you mean you think he may know something about his death?" Miss Frayle glanced at the story about Johnny Destiny's untimely end. Accident, it seemed to suggest. That was how it looked from what the newspaper said. Yet, she thought, there was the reference to Inspector Hood. Would he have been on the job if it were merely an accident?

"I was wondering," she heard Erica say, "that is, do you think I ought to let your Inspector Hood know? About this other man?"

Miss Frayle's eyes behind her horn-rims widened as they met Erica's look, troubled and uncertain, over her cup of coffee.

Chapter Twelve

MISS FRAYLE AND Erica Travers headed along the main street towards the sea-front. After discussing it at length over another cup of coffee Erica had agreed with Miss Frayle that there probably wasn't any real significance to be attached to the fact that she had observed someone watching the man she had met on the boat, whom the newspaper reported to be Johnny Destiny. There was nothing to it that would be worth bringing to the notice of the police, anyway.

"As I say, it was just my imagination," Erica had said. "It certainly didn't seem to bother him, when I mentioned it at the time." And so they had dropped the idea of phoning Inspector Hood, and Erica and Miss Frayle turned their attention to making the most of their visit to Southend, and had hurried from the café to see the sights.

The end of the street fell away into a short, steep incline that led down on to the esplanade. Miss Frayle and Erica paused to fill their lungs with the strong, salty tang that came up off the inshore mudflats which the incoming tide was now covering.

Miss Frayle adjusted her glasses and stared at the milling scene on beach and promenade. Erica had seen it all before, of course, but she was admitting how she never failed to get a kick from watching the Southend holiday scene. The day-trippers from London in their paper hats spilling from the motor-coaches and the excursion-trains to swamp the promenade and beaches, amusement arcades, winkle-shops and ice-cream stalls with their exuberant presence.

Just for a day the invaders had shaken the dust of the city off their feet; they were loosening up, letting their hair down. No one took any notice. Everyone was doing it. Having themselves a good time: men, women and children.

Miss Frayle found it all quite overwhelming. She had seen nothing like it anywhere before. The coaches and cars along the seafront drive, the throngs of people on the promenade and around the pier entrance; men in open neck shirts with red, sun-scorched faces, women in gay cotton frocks with peeling sun-tanned arms, girls in shorts and handkerchief tops with slim brown legs and shoulders eating candy-floss, children in swimsuits, devouring ice-creams or lollipops. The motley of noise and colour made a deep contrast to the solitude of Dormouse Creek.

Privately, Miss Frayle had to confess she preferred the latter by a long way. Above the sound of the laughing, rowdy throng sounded the enticing calls of the boatmen along the beach. Numerous pleasure-boats of varying sizes lay alongside their mobile gang-planks awaiting the tide, while their skippers called out descriptive invitations to sail across the bay or round the pier.

And the pier really was something to sail around. Stretching way out into the estuary of the Thames, its tip almost lost in the hazy dazzle of sun on water. Like a long bridge across a calm sea, flowing with traffic, human and mechanical. Alongside the narrow electric railway, holiday-makers marched, some outward bound and others moving shore-wards. It seemed a long long way to the end and Miss Frayle was not surprised to learn from Erica that it was the longest pleasure pier in the world.

Miss Frayle's fascinated gaze wandered over the beach to her left in the direction of Thorpe Bay. "There's the Kursaal," Erica said. "We must see that, unless you might like to take a trip on the pier first. How about riding to the end, having a snack lunch and taking in the Kursaal this afternoon?"

"I'm in your hands," Miss Frayle said. She realized

Erica was determined in no uncertain style to kill the time they had to spend waiting for Jim Rayner to emerge from his conference. There was nothing she could do except join in.

As they walked towards the pier entrance, Miss Frayle could not help marvelling at the adaptable creature which Erica was. Only yesterday in the elegant atmosphere of Paris, and now here she was all ready to join in the blatant fun and amusement of boisterous Southend.

On the pier Erica led Miss Frayle towards the miniature railway-station. They bought the tickets and went down the steps to the wooden platform. A model train stood waiting and they climbed into one of the observation cars. The train soon filled up and within a few minutes, it moved off out of the station, up on to the top level of the pier.

As it clanged slowly out over the sea, Miss Frayle watched the crowded shore recede with its background of shops and stalls, the cliff behind and its great hotel lording it over all. Erica picked out the Kursaal for her, and then her attention moved further along, following the sweep of the bay towards Shoeburyness, where motor-boats and small sailing-yachts dotted the water. Way out to sea in the deep water, ocean-going steamers passed, some outward bound, others heading up the Thames for London.

On the other side of the train, beyond the rail separating the track from the footway, streams of people mooched along, or sat resting half-way on their journey. Here and there a man stood patiently guarding his fishing-rod, waiting for its alarm-bell to ring and signify a bite. Even in the train the trip seemed quite a distance, but eventually they were slowing to a stop in the seaward terminus.

Erica led the way towards the large cluster of buildings on the pier-head. Suddenly her attention was arrested by a speed-boat.

"Come on," she said. Taking Miss Frayle's arm she was propelling her towards a queue at the top of some steps. "If you haven't been out in a speed-boat before, here's your chance."

Before Miss Frayle realized it, she was allowing herself to be attached to the queue, Erica beside her. Down the steps they went as one boat was pulling away and another came alongside. Miss Frayle heard the motor roar and saw the departing boat lift its flared bows while the stern and the passengers in it disappeared from view behind the twin towers of spray. Miss Frayle turned to Erica anxiously.

"I don't know whether I shall like it," she said.

Erica was laughing excitedly. "It's madly exhilarating, give you a marvellous appetite for lunch."

It was too late to back out, anyway, Miss Frayle decided. They were moving down the steps urged on by those behind, and then she was being helped into the front cockpit of the boat.

"More fun at the back, actually," Erica said as they took their places. "But you do get a bit wet, and you can't see much for spray."

Miss Frayle eyed two giggling girls and a joking young man in the stern, and noticed they had been provided with an oil-skin. She felt thankful to be in the front. Taking on and discharging customers was a slick operation, and almost before Miss Frayle could worry about what was ahead of her they were moving gently away from the landing-stage.

A sudden roar behind her back, the foredeck suddenly leapt in the air, and they were droning across the smooth surface of the sea. Shouts and hysterical laughter from behind, and Miss Frayle glanced round, surprised to find herself looking down on the stern, which seemed a long way down, where the water bubbled and frothed in great feathers of spray about the laughing girls and young man.

Miss Frayle turned back to the salt-caked windscreen. All she could see was the high point of the bows. But Erica was right. The ride was exhilarating. Only when they weaved about, bouncing over their own wash, did her stomach turn right over. The excitement was of short duration. Soon they were heading back to the pier, the boat dropped on an even keel and came alongside the landing-stage.

Erica said when they were on the top deck of the pier again. "Give you a kick?"

Miss Frayle wiped the spray off her glasses.

"It was rather fun," she said. "Though I'm glad it was before lunch, definitely."

They walked as far as the long sun-deck watching the passengers embarking on the Clacton steamer. Holidaymakers lined the rails as she drew away, waving excitedly at those on the pier as though they were about to voyage to the other side of the globe. Amused by the complete abandon of the snoozers in the deck-chairs, by the patience of the fishermen on the lower decks and by the seagulls diving raucously over the children munching cakes or sandwiches, Miss Frayle and Erica made their way to the restaurant.

Following a quick snack, they caught the train back to the shore. The morning had gone so quickly, there was little time left before they would be meeting Jim Rayner again, and Erica was anxious to sample as much as she could of entertainment offered by the Kursaal.

Off the pier they turned towards Thorpe Bay, forcing their way through the jostling crowds on the esplanade. The tide was right up now and children dashed in and out of the water with delighted squeals, or built sand-castles on the few inches of remaining beach. Miss Frayle couldn't remember when she had seen a beach so crowded before. There was hardly room to move between sprawled bodies, deck-chairs and picnic-baskets.

The sight of outstretched figures all shapes and sizes, drying off in their swimsuits, varying in complexion from white to lobster-red and from red to brown reminded Miss Frayle to take care that she didn't catch the sun. She was the type who peeled. Brunette Erica, on the other hand, wasn't likely to suffer. Her skin showed a faint tan already without going through the painful process which in the past had been Miss Frayle's fate.

They crossed to the further pavement, even more crowded than the esplanade, with shops and stalls purveying rock and postcards, whelks and walking-sticks, ice-cream parlours and stalls with great mounds of candy floss, all besieged by children and adults alike. The fortune-teller, the gimmick boy, the balloon man, the novelty stall, all were doing a roaring trade.

Miss Frayle found the way to the Kursaal harder going than window-shopping in Oxford Street, and inside the Kursaal gates she and Erica paused to get their breath.

"We'll certainly need a holiday after this," Erica said. "Thank heavens we can recuperate on the *Moya*."

Miss Frayle eyed the chairplanes, the roundabouts and the dive-bomber beyond. Her ears were assailed with raucous shouts, hysterical screams of laughter. "I'm not going on anything," she said firmly. "That speed-boat was enough for one day."

Erica laughed, and they walked side-by-side into the heart of the funfair.

The same bustle, the same crowds, the same children with ice-cream cornets, clinging to parental hands, only the noise was worse. Now they were in the thick of it Miss Frayle decided it was one great hurdy-gurdy of music, guffaws and grinding metal, the exhortations of the barkers and stall-holders.

She stared at the aeroplanes circling over her head until she was dizzy; how anyone could retain consciousness in the dive-bomber? There was the crack of air-rifles, the rattle of skittles and coconut-shies, the swings and the water-chute. Less nerve-racking was the entertainment offered by the hoop-la, the darts and rolling the penny.

It was near a fortune-teller's tent that Erica stopped, her sudden grip on Miss Frayle's arm was so fierce that Miss Frayle turned to her in alarm.

"What is it?" Anxiously she followed the other's gaze riveted on a man who was approaching.

Erica seemed too stunned to answer. Miss Frayle stared at the man. He wore a light, rather flashy-looking suit, a dark shirt and a light tie. She thought the face under the pearl grey hat might be vaguely familiar, but she couldn't place it. He turned away and was lost in the milling throng. "You saw him," Erica whispered.

"Yes," Miss Frayle said, frowning. "But —"

"It's him, the man whose photo's in the paper."

Miss Frayle eyed her incredulously. "You mean, the man —? But — it can't be, he's dead."

Erica was gasping, as if she had been running. "I know it's him," she said. "It's Johnny Destiny."

As she spoke she began moving in the direction the man had taken, Miss Frayle, completely at a loss, tagging after her.

Chapter Thirteen

DEAF TO THE noise about him, oblivious of the mob, he mooched around the sideshows, his attention concentrated on the object of his search, that which had attracted him like a magnet to this boisterous, rumbustious carnival beneath the blazing afternoon sun.

He paused for a moment by a rifle range watching the mugs take aim. One man reminded him slightly of the man yesterday. The thin mouth beneath the light snap-brim cracked in a faint, inward smile. It was okay so many people did have some superficial resemblance to one another. Or maybe he should have been forced to lay low for a while to grow a moustache.

Seeing yourself staring out of the newsprint, like he had seen himself this morning had rated as quite a shock with him. Especially when the story that went with your mug reported you dead. That was what made him feel he was in the clear. The cold fact there in black and white and his passport-photo. It was a million to one chance he'd be spotted. It was psychological. Plus that it wasn't a good passport-photo of him anyway.

He moved slowly, casually, keeping close to the stalls, giving each girl he passed a careful once-over. The girl was here somewhere, he wanted to waste as little time as possible locating her.

He found her at a hoop-la stall.

He was certain it was her. A dark, sulky beauty with eyes like shining pools and lustrous black hair. Gold earrings against a soft white neck. That was what he was looking at now, in person. If the photograph he had remembered erred at all, it was only that it was more luscious in the flesh.

He stood back, watching and waiting.

He liked watching her; but he liked what lay beyond her, what was waiting for him at the end of his trip much better. He didn't wish to draw any attention to himself. There came a bit of a lull around her stall, and he moved in just like any other mug.

"Here y'are, sir." She held out a cluster of coloured hoops. "Seven for six, fourteen for a shilling."

Ernest Dudley

Johnny gave her a shilling and went through the motions. He aimed at the upended box of chocolates on its wooden stand and after half a dozen attempts managed to ring it clearly. He got through the rest of the hoops without any further luck.

She brought him the box of chocolates. He decided she looked at him in a way that suggested she didn't mind what she saw. "You've been lucky," she said.

"Must be you," he said, with his most inviting smile. "I never had much luck at games."

She rose to it. She came in on cue. It wasn't new stuff to her. It was pretty old hat. "Perhaps you're lucky in love," she said.

"Guess I missed out on that, too. The candy's for you."

"What about my figure?" she said.

"You really want to know what about it?" he said.

"Why, you an expert?"

"I'll call back later and give you a demonstration," he said. "Say, around closing time?"

She shrugged. Her eyes were bold. She stared at him frankly, unblinkingly. "May not be many chocolates left by then."

He grinned at her. He'd hardly ever had it so easy.

"Who should I ask for?"

"Lucilla."

"Nice name," he said. That was the name he had remembered her by. It was her okay. He hadn't made any mistake. His pulses raced a little in excited triumph. He took out a packet of cigarettes and offered her one. She didn't smoke while she was working. He lit a cigarette for himself and took a deep drag at it. His eyes glinted at her through the smoke.

"You're an American," she said.

He nodded. "Hoop-la," he said. "Hollywood talent-scout, you got any talent?"

"That old stuff," she said derisively.

"Well," he said, "if I told you the truth, you wouldn't wear it."

A mob was pushing round him, and the girl had to go into her routine. He grinned at her again and said he'd be back all right, and she stared after him for a moment until he'd vanished in the crowd.

It was strange the impression he'd made on her. She'd handled the fast customers before; she knew the backchat to give the boys on the make.

Even though they were the customers, and always right, she knew how to keep them in their place.

She'd never let any of them date her. But he was different. He had a way with him. She wondered if he really would come back. Maybe, if he was lonely. An American serviceman on leave in the town, and alone.

She couldn't help hoping he would come back. He was a fast worker and no mistake. But then these Yanks were like that. She recalled some joke she'd heard about them. What was it? Over-paid, over-sexed, and over here, that was the joke. She smiled to herself. Not that he'd seemed like that. A bit over-dressed, perhaps, but it suited him. And he wasn't loud and cocky. Quiet, and with a sense of humour.

A girl who somehow didn't look the type to play hoopla was pushing her way to the stall, with another young woman behind her, fair-haired with horn-rimmed glasses. She leaned forward automatically, waving a fist full of hoops.

"No, thanks," Erica Travers said to her, then hesitated, before she said: "Frankly I wondered if you could tell me who that man was you were speaking to?"

Lucilla drew herself up, her eyes bright with resentment. "I haven't a clue who he was," she said. "And if I did, why should I tell you? Why don't you chase after him and then you can ask him yourself?"

"It's not that," Erica said quickly. "It — it's only that I thought I knew him. And since he was talking to you —"

Lucilla shook her head. Some kind of alarm-bell had suddenly rung faintly at the back of her mind. "He was just a customer," she said. "Never seen him before."

"I see," Erica Travers said.

She turned to Miss Frayle behind her, who gazed at her questioningly and then back at the girl at the stall. The mob pushed and perspired around them. But Miss Frayle knew that Erica was reluctant to leave without obtaining more information concerning the man she'd seen and whom they'd followed, only to lose him again after they'd seen him talking to this dark girl. This girl who obviously resented being asked about him.

Erica turned back from Miss Frayle to the girl at the hoop-la again. Her expression was determined, but she managed to force a coaxing smile into her question.

"You — that is — you don't know his name?" she said.

"No."

"I mean, he didn't say who he was?"

"I heard you the first time. It's still no, I don't know him."

"It wasn't Destiny? Johnny Destiny?"

Suddenly Lucilla felt scared. She didn't know why, and she covered up her unreasoning fear with a burst of ill-temper. "Haven't I just told you?" she said. "He didn't tell me who he was." And she turned away with her hoopla rings to answer the demands of the throng that had deepened as it milled round her. She didn't look to see what the brunette and the fair one in the specs did about it. She didn't care.

Chapter Fourteen

TOGETHER WITH HIS opponent facing him, Dr. Morelle sank on his knees and bowed low, until his forehead touched the tatami, the rice-straw mattress with its shining surface, in the age-old ritual of the contest, which is more than a trial of strength, or the matching of skill and wills, but is a contest between philosophers' minds.

Chief instructor of the Judo Club, dark-haired, thickset little Welshman, Griffiths, got to his feet, and Dr. Morelle followed suit, giving a hitch to his white jacket around which he wore the black belt of a fourth Dan. His opponent similarly attired was a seventh Dan, with several years' experience at the Kodokwan in Tokyo.

It was late afternoon, the Dojo or club-room, in the centre of which the two men prepared to practice their science, was a lofty-ceilinged room with the tall windows overlooking the side-street which led off the Cromwell Road. The windows were wide open to the light summer breeze.

Griffiths moved in, with his right hand extended, elbow tucked close, as if pointing a gun.

With a swift movement Dr. Morelle pushed the V formed by the thumb and fingers of his left hand, with the thumb pointed downwards, against the other's extended wrist, and forced it to the left. In the same movement he advanced his left foot diagonally to the left, and now with his right hand caught Griffiths' hand which held the imaginary gun.

Keeping both his arms straight Dr. Morelle made a left turn on the ball of his left foot, swinging his opponent's captured arm over his head. He shifted his right foot to correct his balance while he straightened Griffiths' arm, pulling his wrist down past his right side, while at the same time he turned the opponent's wrist to the right.

Griffiths opened his right hand as if releasing the gun.

The little Welshman grinned at him.

"Nice, Doctor," he said. "If I'd had my finger on the trigger guard of the gun you'd have torn my hand to bits."

Dr. Morelle shook his head in self-criticism. "Not half-fast enough," he said. "That's what comes of being unable to keep up one's training. You lose the split-second coordination which in an emergency could make all the difference."

"Don't forget," the other said, "that in such a case, chances are you'd be dealing not with an expert, but with someone who wouldn't know the first thing about Judo."

Dr. Morelle gave him a nod. "Nevertheless," he said, "one should be prepared for an opponent who knows more than you do."

The Dojo remained empty for the next hour, the club-members usually did not arrive until early evening, and Dr. Morelle and Griffiths went through a dozen exercises, practising the moves and holds, the shifts and stratagems which would be required to deal with an attempted hold-up by an armed assailant.

Perspiration poured down their faces and bared chests as they circled and lunged, parried and struck, the soles of their bare feet a sibilant hiss on the shining surface of the tatami. Dr. Morelle defended himself against a drunk swinging punches at him. As Griffiths in the role of a drunken attacker flung out his left fist Dr. Morelle's right forearm blocked the blow, while his left hand gripped the other's right wrist, pushing it back to the left. He moved left with his left foot, and brought his right foot past his opponent's right foot, grabbing the other's right elbow with his right hand, at the same time bringing his left foot behind Griffiths, to pin his wrists between his shoulder-blades. Pressing down on the other's right elbow, Dr. Morelle now had his own left elbow forced hard against Griffiths' left shoulder-blade, his feet were placed so that he was perfectly balanced, his knees bent and relaxed.

"Okay, Dr. Morelle," Griffiths said, and they relaxed.

They left the tatami to sit squatted against the white-painted wall, while they discussed Judo, its origins and philosophy.

"Let's hope, of course," Griffiths was saying, "you don't have to prove my words, but I really think there's not many you'd meet who'd stand much chance against you."

"Win your battle with the sword in its sheath, eh?" Dr. Morelle said.

"That's the way they say it in Japan," the other said. "If you can talk your way out of trouble without having to demonstrate how smart a jujitsu expert you are, so much the wiser."

"A man can be a Black Belt," Dr. Morelle said, "without necessarily being a great philosopher. But all things being equal — health and physique — a great philosopher would almost certainly have the makings of a Black Belt."

The dark-haired Welshman nodded. "It's like the noise which follows the clap of the hands," he said. "You can't have one without the other. For one's body to be so coordinated that it automatically takes control as required in the face of danger, that is the height of achievement for the jujitsu exponent."

"Which perfection," Dr. Morelle said, "requires continuous practice." He gave a little sigh. "I fear that much as I wish I were able to give the science more time, life holds too many distractions for me to be able to do so."

"Maybe," Griffiths said, "but you don't do so badly." He regarded Dr. Morelle's lean profile while he noted that his breathing was steady and regular, the deep chest between the wide angular shoulders rose and fell rhythmically. "I suppose it's because you possess such terrific powers of concentration which few people have."

"You're very kind," Dr. Morelle said. "In fact, my work does require a certain amount of application in order to attain any measure of success."

He seemed about to enlarge upon the subject, when he turned his head quickly as a shadow darkened the doorway to the Dojo. The familiar figure that had appeared there and now stood looking across at him brought the faintest shadow of a frown to Dr. Morelle's aquiline features.

"Hope I'm not intruding," Detective-Inspector Hood of New Scotland Yard said, with a slow grin spreading beneath his iron-grey moustache. He was wearing a well-worn pin-stripe suit of conservative cut and carried a bowler hat. He made as if to step forward onto the tatami when he was halted by a peremptory word.

"Wait," Dr. Morelle said. He got to his feet and his companion also stood up as he padded across. "Against the rules," Dr. Morelle said, "to walk on the tatami in your shoes." The detective wore an expression of puzzled amusement. "If you knew anything about the science to which this place is dedicated you'd appreciate that you spend some considerable amount of your time with your face on the floor. That's why we're careful to prevent dirt being brought in from the street."

"Oh," Inspector Hood said, and a trifle self-consciously he took the blackened briar pipe he was chewing on from between his teeth and pushed it into his pocket. "Miss Frayle said you might be here," he said.

Dr. Morelle's eyebrow shot up, and a look of pain flitted across his saturnine features, glistening with sweat. "She would," he said uncompromisingly. "From which it requires little difficulty to deduce that you have only recently had the dubious pleasure of conversation with her."

Dr. Morelle had led Inspector Hood out of the Dojo and along the passage to a corner where they could talk undisturbed. They made an incongruous pair, Dr. Morelle, lean, sinewy and glowing as a result of his work-out, in his white jacket and short trousers, and the man from Scotland Yard heavily-built in his formal suit, and bowler hat clutched in his thick hands.

Miss Frayle had seen the force of Erica Travers' suggestion that they ought to get in touch with Inspector Hood. But she could not help wishing that they had not been involved themselves in this business. All very well for Erica to satisfy her curiosity, but another thing to make your interest known to a third party. If the girl at the hoop-la knew that it was Johnny Destiny she wasn't likely to give him away, and Erica's inquiries might incur some risk to herself by warning the man that she had recognized him.

Mingled with her uneasiness was the feeling in her own mind that Erica had made a mistake. It was putting too much faith in a newspaper photograph to rely on it as proof of identity. On the other hand though, Erica had met the man; she had been in his company only the day before, on the boat.

It was then that she decided that the best thing to do was not to get in touch with Inspector Hood, but speak to Dr. Morelle about it. That way, following Dr. Morelle's advice, she and Erica could return to Dormouse Creek and carry on with their holiday in peace.

But she was to be thwarted in achieving this simple solution to her problem. In the call-box outside the Kursaal she listened with Erica beside her to the distant burr-burr of the telephone ringing at 221b Harley Street. The ringing was not answered. It was then that Miss Frayle, glancing at her watch, realized that Dr. Morelle had said something about the Judo Club. She considered getting him there, she didn't know the number, but the Directory would give it her, but decided that it mightn't be such a good idea. She might not find him in a very receptive mood. Miss Frayle, with Erica's agreement, settled for Inspector Hood, after all.

"I thought you were on holiday, Miss Frayle," Inspector Hood had said to her, when she finally got through to him at Scotland Yard. She plunged into her explanation for telephoning him.

"It's about a friend of mine, Miss Travers, I'm on holiday with her, she's sure she's seen the man whose body was found on the boat-train at

Victoria yesterday. You know, the newspapers say his name's Johnny Destiny."

Inspector Hood had heard her out. Prompted by Erica she told him all she knew. "And what do you think, Miss Frayle?" he said, his tone noncommittal.

"I suppose he could resemble the photo in the paper," she said slowly. "But it might be just coincidence. But, Erica, Miss Travers, is positive that he's the same man she met on the boat."

As Inspector Hood related all this that Miss Frayle had told him over the phone now to Dr. Morelle, he unconsciously produced his pipe again from his pocket and chewed its stem. "What do you think of it?" he said finally. He searched the gaunt, aquiline features that had been bent upon him attentively. Both Inspector Hood and Dr. Morelle had made their respective contribution towards the unravelling of the tangled skein that had been the Transatlantic case, and the name of Johnny Destiny was something to be reckoned with.

"Of course," the detective said dubiously, "it's easy enough to make a mistake in the crowds at Southend Kursaal. And, I mean, he was found on the train all right, and after all, when a chap's dead, he's dead."

Dr. Morelle regarded him with a faintly mocking expression. He could hear the thwack from the Dojo of a body meeting the tatami as Griffiths and another member of the Judo Club engaged in a bout.

"It would appear that this one isn't," he said.

Chapter Fifteen

HE WAS PLEASED with himself. He was riding high, like on the roller-coaster at the Kursaal. He'd found the girl, and she was all ready to move right in under his umbrella.

Any fear back of his mind that she might have left the place was wiped out as soon as he saw the hoop-la stall. He'd made a good impression, she was ready to go for him. But then didn't he find it went that way with any number he had wanted to go for him? He smiled thinly to himself and went into one of the Kursaal snack-bars and ordered coffee and hot dogs.

He didn't notice the other customers. He sat at the counter in a corner. He began working it out he was going to play his hand from here. He had to be diplomatic. No use pushing her and setting the fire-alarm ringing. He'd got to take it gently and he was sure she'd lead him home. Casual inquiries about where she came from, was she alone, she have any folk around?

If he played his cards right, an hour or so with her should put him on the road to his final destination. He would be glad to get out of Southend, anyway. Hot and crowded and noisy, it was unwise to stay in any one place too long. And this crummy place was no place to stay anyway. He rode the electric train to the pier-head, found a chair in a quiet corner in the shade and relaxed. It was nice just to lie back with his eyes closed and feel the gentle sea breeze whispering across his face. Nice just to lie there, and think of nothing in particular, knowing everything was organized up to date.

He was back on shore again by seven. He wandered along towards Westcliff, lingering over a couple of drinks in a bar. When he returned to the Kursaal he was still feeling good and all set to click the last cog in the works into place.

She was trying to look as though she wasn't waiting for him at the hoop-la. The customers were still throwing the rings, but there was another girl working the stall. The dark, sultry girl saw him and said something to the other girl. The other girl glanced up in his direction and smirked. He gave Lucilla a glad hand, then she came out to meet him.

She looked more attractive now than when he had first seen her. Luscious was the word. She'd changed her frock. He could see it wasn't an expensive one. Just a plain summery job with a full skirt and an off-the-shoulder line, but she looked a million in it. She didn't wear much make-up. A touch of lipstick to turn her full mouth to a deeper red.

"I wondered if you'd be back," she said. The glance from beneath her dark mascarad eyelashes held a conversation with his own eyes.

"I didn't," he said. "Nothing could have kept me away."

She eyed him sceptically, but she fell into step beside him and he took her arm, and she changed her handbag over so that it didn't bang against him.

"How much busier than this can you get?" His glance took in the crowds still milling around.

She laughed softly. "What about your Coney Island?" she said. "From what I've heard, this place is an old folks' home, compared. You been to Coney Island?"

He nodded. "I've been there. It's bigger than this. Like a city all on its own. Theatres, night-clubs, all the works. Sure it's different from this. But this is okay." His pale eyes glinted at her from under the brim of his light hat. "Let's get out of here, and have a drink," he said.

They left the Kursaal and walked along the front towards the pier. Off the Western Esplanade they found a small bar. It was quieter than most, though the shouts and clamour of the holiday-makers still came to them as they sat down. A couple of drinks, then they moved on up the cliff to a hotel he had earmarked earlier. He bought her a good dinner. There was a bottle of champagne and it brought a sparkle to her lustrous eyes. The warm glow of her reached across the table and encircled him.

She began talking about herself. He already knew part of her story. But she didn't know he knew. She didn't know he knew more about her than she did herself. Her mother had died when she was a kid. She'd been alone a lot. She'd had to make her own way from the time she'd left school. Her father had drifted abroad. Vague business ventures, she said, she didn't know much about that, had sent him travelling all over Europe. His expression didn't change while she told him this. She'd never seen much of her father until now, she said. She was thankful he'd settled down at last.

A lonely inn on the marshes. He made a living from it. That and a bit on the side, shooting wildfowl. It was not far from Southend and she could keep an eye on him. She went over there as often as she could. It wasn't everybody's cup of tea. But she liked it and so did the old man.

Things were moving his way, already they were moving his way, he was telling himself. The inn not far away, that was how it was going to be, was it? He didn't need much more and he'd have it all fixed. Working like this, with the big notion in the forefront of his mind, helped him keep his thoughts away from the romantic excursion the girl opposite invited. But she was a baby he could take to.

They finished their coffee. He had a brandy, but she still had a little of her champagne left to sip. She smoked one of his American cigarettes, he tapped it out of the packet for her. He bought himself a cigar, Havana. She watched him light it with admiration. Presently they strolled out of the hotel and wandered into the cliff gardens close by. The lights stringing along the promenade and pier glittered against the haze of the close of the summer's day. Still the noise of crowds, and from somewhere the sound of dance-music. But it was quieter in the gardens, it seemed a way away. They were alone among trees and shrubbery and the scent of flowers.

They found a seat in the shadows of a tree. His arm moved round her shoulders and he felt her faint shiver as his fingers touched her flesh. She snuggled closer to him, and he kissed her ear.

"Been a swell evening, hon," he said. "Couldn't we dream up some more like this one?"

"Only me and you to stop us," she said. Her voice was a languorous whisper.

"To-morrow?"

She hesitated uncertainly. "I should be going over to see my father."

"Has he got room for a weary traveller," he said.

She drew out of his arm to stare at him. Her eyes were bright pools of wonder in the dusk. "You wouldn't want to come over with me?"

"Nothing I'd like better than to tag along." His words came out warm and fast, there was a deep note of sincerity, old-fashioned stuff, so that he could have been wanting to ask her father for his daughter's hand in marriage. "You know something, hon," he said. "You made where he hangs out sound like sweet music to me. Somewhere to get away from crowds and noise." He paused, and then he packed the real throb into it. "Somewhere where we could be really alone."

"I'm sure you wouldn't like it," she said. "You'd think it was just some dump, I mean. And it's miles from anywhere."

"You got me figured out wrong, hon, when you say that," he said. She was in his arms again. His mouth was against her ear. "The backwoods stuff is for me. If you knew how much I wanted to cut away from civilization, if only for a while. Get right back to Doctor Nature. And your pop's place sounds just what the doc ordered. If you want to go over there to-morrow for as long as you want, it's okay by me. Just so long as I'm right by your side."

It was easier than he had expected. He arranged to pick her up in a car he'd hired at the room she had in a side-street not far from the Kursaal next afternoon. She said she could organize it so that she wouldn't have to return until the day after next. She was sure her father would put him up all right. They stayed on, lost in the deepening shadows of the tree. He could give her the business now. His mind was temporarily free from the big caper, he could concentrate on the romantic stuff which was expected of him. It wasn't difficult to ease himself into the mood. The night was close, filled with the scent of flowers. The sound of the traffic had faded into a distant murmur, mingled with voices of holiday-makers drifting past. Somewhere far away the red and green navigation lights on the ships in the estuary flickered in the darkness.

And Lucilla wasn't at all unwilling.

It was late when they left the gardens. Down on the esplanade things were quieter, though they met more people near the pier. Then they were in a quiet street that lay behind the Kursaal, and it was outside the house where she had her room that she suddenly pulled herself out of his good-night embrace. He glanced at her curiously.

"I clean forgot," she said. "I must be out of my mind."

"What is it?"

He was grinning at her in the darkness of the silent street. But she wasn't smiling. "That damned girl," she said. Her eyes snapped at the memory. And she had meant to tell him the first moment she'd seen him again, and then she had completely forgotten it once in his company. "It was just after you left the hoop-la this afternoon."

"What was?"

He wasn't particularly interested.

"This girl." She glanced at his face shadowed by his grey hat, hesitated. She didn't want to spoil their evening. Then she shrugged, it was probably nothing. "She said she thought she knew you. She'd seen you with me."

He mightn't have heard her, he mightn't have been listening. He appeared as relaxed and casual as ever.

"What did you say?" he said. She didn't catch the grating note in his voice.

"There was another one with her. She was wearing glasses. I said I didn't know you. It was the truth." She smiled at him lovingly. "I didn't — then."

"What else she say?"

"She asked me if your name was Destiny. Johnny Destiny. I gave her the same answer. I didn't know you, I said."

"Who's he?" he said. He had given her the name under which he booked at the hotel in Southend, where he'd managed to get himself fixed up.

"Search me," she said, and clung to him again, her mouth seeking his.

This had hit him like a bolt out of the blue, but he was smiling at her, his arms about her were holding her close, as if there was nothing else in the world that mattered. It could be some sharp-eyed piece had recognized him from his photo in the newspaper. But it seemed incredible, to have spotted him in all that mob, he didn't believe it. Yet how else? He needed to find out a bit more about this girl who'd recognized him.

"She'd got me mixed up with someone else, I guess," he said. "I don't know any girl who wears glasses."

"It wasn't her. She was just a friend, she stayed in the background. The girl was dark and pretty. She asked about you."

"Only pretty girl I know in the whole wide world is you," he said. "The only girl I want to know."

She loved it; while his thoughts were chasing around his brain like a whirlpool of daggers. A dark-haired pretty girl who knew him? He couldn't tie it up, however he tried. It would have to be somebody he'd met in the last two days, it was his first time over here in years. But there was no one. He'd barely spoken to a soul, since he'd arrived. It must have been some girl gimlet-eye, after all. It just went to prove how careful you had to be. From the passport-photo in the newspaper. It had to be, had to be that. Since Paris, who'd there been? Why, if you like, take it since —?

It was then he remembered the girl on the boat, and the stabbing-question-marks racing round inside his skull began to ease up. The brunette on the cross-Channel steamer, he'd chinned with her. The image of her formed on his mind.

And hadn't she said something about she was meeting some friend for a holiday in Essex?

85

Chapter Sixteen

THERE WAS JUST enough breeze to rustle the sedge grass on the other side of Dormouse Creek. The morning sun shone fiercely out of a brilliantly blue sky, and across the marsh isolated pools of water shimmered placidly. In the meadow beyond the Wildfowler Inn, cattle moved slowly across to the boundary ditch and stood in the sparse shade of the trees swishing at the flies with their tails.

Lying on the rug spread out on the deck Miss Frayle glimpsed the white sail approaching, and she sat up to look at it further. She pointed it out to Erica who was lying beside her, face down, sunning her back and legs. Grumbling at being disturbed, Erica raised herself and stared down the creek. It was a small sloop and she recognized its dark blue hull and low easy lines. "It's Jim," she said. "In a job he borrows from Burnham."

Miss Frayle looked with increased interest at the oncoming vessel. She was feeling extremely sophisticated in her swimsuit, Erica had eyed her enviously and that was no faint praise, coming from her. Miss Frayle had wondered if perhaps it wasn't a bit too much for the rustic environment of Dormouse Creek, but she had received full encouragement from Erica, who wore a much more revealing two-piece affair, and Aunt Edith: "Do the local yokels a bit of good to have an eye-opener." So Miss Frayle had gone to work on her shoulders and legs with sun-tan oil.

The appearance of the white-sailed boat would give Miss Frayle an opportunity of assessing her swimsuit's impact upon a masculine mentality. Not that Jim Rayner was a local yokel. Miss Frayle couldn't quite decide whether Erica liked or disliked him. But then she had always invariably referred to her young men acquaintances in somewhat disparaging terms, which you didn't take too seriously. She had given the impression that she thought Jim Rayner was a bit of a dope, but really she seemed to be quite fond of him.

"Don't worry about him," Erica was saying now, as she relaxed again, face downwards on the deck. "He won't be aboard for a while."

Miss Frayle relaxed and allowed her mind to drift into speculation about the result of her telephone-call yesterday afternoon to Inspector Hood. Had he got in touch with Dr. Morelle, as he had said he would? She thought it was certain he had, but she couldn't for the life of her decide what Dr. Morelle's reaction to the story she had given the Scotland Yard man would be. He might have dismissed it as another example of her lurid imagination, as he had more than once described it, running riot. And Miss Frayle gave a wry smile to herself as she pictured Dr. Morelle advising Inspector Hood that he was wasting both his and the latter's time. Yet Inspector Hood had not sounded at all unimpressed over the phone. Far from it. And Miss Frayle knew how Dr. Morelle was no less interested in Johnny Destiny than the other. Johnny Destiny and the Transatlantic business.

And then she thought: supposing Dr. Morelle decided to take a serious view of what she'd told Inspector Hood? There was no reason why she should hear any more about it, not until the news appeared in the newspapers that Johnny Destiny had been caught, at any rate. She had done her part, there was nothing else she could do. It was in Scotland Yard's and Dr. Morelle's hands now, it wasn't likely either of them would think it necessary to interrupt her and Erica's holiday to demand their help. If Dr. Morelle did get in touch with her at all about it, it would be merely to advise her to forget the matter and leave her mind free to continue with her holiday.

Miss Frayle saw the sailing-boat draw nearer to the *Moya*. She observed Erica raise her pretty dark head again to watch it with a casual eye. She reflected that Jim Rayner, who had heard all about it over tea in the café where he'd been awaiting them yesterday afternoon, and Aunt Edith when they'd returned to the *Moya*, had both thought Erica and Miss Frayle had acted misguidedly at the Kursaal.

Both had agreed it was perfectly obvious that Erica had been mistaken. "To be able to pick out some chap in that mob as someone you met briefly the day before — you've been seeing things," had been Jim Rayner's verdict. And it had been echoed by Aunt Edith, despite Erica's profound conviction that she hadn't been mistaken, backed up by Miss Frayle's opinion that there had seemed to have been a resemblance between the man at the hoop-la and the newspaper photo.

Miss Frayle would have admitted that Erica's memory had played her tricks, and then she recalled how Inspector Hood had sounded over the phone. As if he was really interested in what she was telling him, almost as if he was already in possession of some knowledge which was linked with her account. Or had he simply been humouring her?

The sailing-boat was passing and Miss Frayle raised her head to obtain a closer glimpse of it through the *Moya's* rails. The boat had a tiny cabin-top which was surrounded by a cat-walk of a deck, and was trailing a pram dinghy. The safest and largest section of it, it seemed to her, was the cockpit. Jim Rayner was in swimming-trunks, and sat on the coaming with the tiller in his hand. He waved as he went by, calling chattily to Erica and Miss Frayle about the weather and giving them a pretty searching look. Erica muttered to the effect that there would be no more peace that morning, and she and Miss Frayle stood up to watch the sailing-boat put about and glide gently downstream towards them. Jim Rayner came aboard the *Moya* with a coloured bathing-towel round his bronzed shoulders.

"Thought you'd take a dip with a lifeguard around," he said. "Already been in and can recommend it."

"Some lifeguard," Erica said.

"I don't think I will," Miss Frayle said. She glanced over the side. The water didn't appear to her to be particularly clear. Besides, although she could swim a bit, it was much too deep.

"Not here," Jim said easily. "Too much mud. Thought of taking you down to the Dormouse."

"The Dormouse?" Miss Frayle said.

"It's a sandy strip near the mouth of the creek," Erica explained. "Much nicer to bathe from there, clear water."

"It's covered a couple of hours either side of high water," Jim said. "But it's ideal at this state of the tide. No mud or barnacles to tread on, just clean firm sand."

Erica had already slipped into the deckhouse and reappeared with two bathing towels. Immediately afterwards Aunt Edith came on deck with her canvas shopping bag, and pausing before going ashore was full of enthusiasm for the idea of a dip from the Dormouse. With the scales thus weighed against her Miss Frayle reluctantly took a towel and she, Erica and Jim made their way along to the jetty ladder where the yacht lay alongside.

Miss Frayle stepped into the cockpit and Jim Rayner's arms, he had gone aboard first. He indicated the side seat and turned to help aboard Erica, and then pushed off. "Heads down," and the mainsail-boom swung across. The sails filled and they moved slowly over the tide down the creek.

"Sort yourselves out," Jim said, cleating home the jib sheet and settling down on the aft coaming with the tiller and the mainsheet. He smiled at Miss Frayle and she blushed a little beneath his gaze which ranged over her figure. She thought she detected a glint in his eyes and decided that it didn't need Dr. Morelle to deduce that her swimsuit was a success.

"Slide along here, Miss Frayle," he said. "Rest your back against this coaming."

She did so, and somehow his hand seemed to find its way on her shoulder. Erica had made a cushion of her towel and was sitting on it, her arm resting on the cabin-top. Miss Frayle took up her towel. "I'll put this round my shoulders," she said. "They've had quite enough sun this morning."

"Sensible idea," Jim said, helping her to drape the towel.

The creek twisted through the marsh, gradually widening as it neared the river into which it flowed. Dark brown mud sloped down into the water from the grass-covered walls on either side. When they went close to the edge of the channel Miss Frayle could see the bottom with here and there large stones to which streamers of green weed clung, swaying to and fro in the eddies like tentacles.

"There's the Dormouse," Erica said, pointing ahead as they rounded the last turn in the creek. Miss Frayle saw a thin strip of gleaming sand just left of the centre of the creek. The water broke all round it in dazzling ripples. Beyond it was the river. The eastern bank of the creek curved round to follow the river at a point parallel to the tip of the Dormouse, but on the western side the wall continued and curved outwards like a mole before following the river upstream. This formed a little bay which sheltered part of the sand strip from the west.

"We'll put her nose on the bar," Jim said as they sailed in towards it. "Breeze is light enough to go in all standing." He moved into the cabin. "I'll get the plate up." Miss Frayle saw him pick up the end of a rope.

Erica was looking at him.

"You mean you're going to run aground?"

"That's where she spends most of her time when I'm ditch-crawling. What she's built for. Sits on the mud like a duck."

"What's the plate you're talking about?" Miss Frayle said, intrigued.

"Centre plate," he said, pointing towards the floor of the cabin, and by leaning forward Miss Frayle could just see the top of a slim wooden case protruding upwards from the floor. "It's a kind of movable metal keel that swivels up and down. It's down now so that we don't make too much leeway. When you're running before the wind or anchored or sailing in shoal waters, you haul it up and it's housed in that case. This job draws only one-foot-six with the plate up, so I can go practically anywhere where there's a cupful of water."

"What a wonderful idea," Miss Frayle said.

Suddenly Jim began to haul on his ropes. There was the squeal of a pulley-block and then the sound of metal against metal as he pinned the plate home. The next moment the nose of the boat slid into the sand and they slowed to a stop. Jim jumped up on to the side deck and juggled with the halyards against the mast and Erica and Miss Frayle were almost smothered in white canvas as the mainsail came down. Soon it was neatly folded along the boom, the jib was stowed and Jim took the anchor and dropped it into the sand.

In the novelty of the sail and excitement of running aground on this tiny island Miss Frayle had forgotten she was still wearing her glasses. It was Erica who reminded her and who put them safely in a locker in the cockpit. They took off their sandals and left them there, too, and Miss Frayle felt the warm, firm sand squeezing through her toes.

Jim Rayner led the way to the narrower channel that ran between the Dormouse and the western bank of the creek. This was also the more shallow channel of the two, where the incoming tide was least felt. The water was warm and Miss Frayle regretted only that they had not come sooner, it was an ideal spot.

It was nearly an hour later when they headed back to the *Moya*. Miss Frayle sat, her towel wrapped round her, in the cockpit. The companion doors and hatch were open so that she could see into the cabin.

She was surprised at the spacious impression it gave. There were two full-length berths with shelves above and lockers underneath. Although the centreboard case broke into the floor space it also served as a support for the folding table, hinged to the mast. Just by the companion there was a cupboard and lockers to starboard and a galley to port with a pressure-stove swinging on gimbals. On the forward bulkhead was a clock, bookshelves, and an oil-lamp and on the locker in the corner a miniature radio-set. An opening in the centre leading through into the fo'c'sle was covered by a curtain. It was cosy enough, but of course, there was no headroom. Miss Frayle knew that if she stood up suddenly she would crash her head on the cabin roof beams.

It was the sight of a solitary figure of a man they passed trudging along the wall of the creek, with a gun under his arm that set Miss Frayle's thoughts revolving around the image she still held in her mind of the limping man in the rainswept, old churchyard. Why, she mused to herself couldn't she stop placing such importance to it? It had been an eerie incident, of course, but it was only because of the somewhat macabre surroundings and gloomy circumstances which had caused her to feel about it as she had. The man had as much right to be there as she and Erica had. And why shouldn't he shelter in what remained of the building as Erica and herself had done in the church porch? As for his furtive manner, that had been nothing more than her imagination. And yet she couldn't shake off that funny feeling she'd had about it. Even now, in the sun, Miss Frayle shivered.

"Cold?" Erica said, from the cabin. "Thought I saw you shiver." Miss Frayle shook her head and smiled. Erica popped her head through the hatch, looking for'ard towards the jetty. "We're nearly there," she said. She came up into the cockpit and sat next to Miss Frayle as the boat heeled in towards the jetty.

Jim Rayner pushed the tiller with his knee and the vessel turned into the breeze. He needed to Erica. "Take the helm," he said, and as she obeyed, he went for'ard to the mast. After a few moments struggling with the halyard he muttered something to the effect that it was jammed. They began to lose way and drift on towards the jetty.

At the same moment Miss Frayle's attention was attracted by a car, a yellow rakish-looking open convertible which was pulling up by the jetty. Her eyes saucer-like behind her glasses she stepped up on to the side-deck for a better view. It was then that Jim managed to get the halyard released. The mainsail came down with a run, its stiff canvas folds falling across Miss Frayle's back and shoulders. Involuntarily she stepped out of the way, the wrong way. With a squeal of dismay she went feet first into the water.

She surfaced quickly, thankful to find her horn-rims still in place and swam to the steps a yard or two away. As she reached the top of the ladder, her hair bedraggled and dripping with water, a familiar figure came into view, to stare down at her sardonically.

"My dear Miss Frayle," Dr. Morelle said, "I thought one always dived in head first."

Chapter Seventeen

IT WAS AT Inspector Hood's suggestion that he and Dr. Morelle had later that afternoon gone along from the Judo Club to B Division police headquarters in Lucan Place, just off the Fulham Road, for a talk with Detective Superintendent "Spider" Bruce.

There was no doubt that the case of the body in the boat-train had assumed proportions somewhat different from what had at first appeared. In the taxi on their way to Chelsea, Inspector Hood had summed up for Dr. Morelle's benefit the conclusions reached by "Spider" Bruce and Superintendent Harper, as a result of probing more deeply into the discovery at Victoria Station.

During the day no reports had come in from anyone, train-drivers or others, on the railway system between London and Folkestone that suggested that the corpse had met its death resulting from looking out of the railway-compartment window. This lack of any confirmatory evidence of any accident at an appropriate time or place helped to confirm the rising suspicion that the death had not ensued from accidental causes. That left only one alternative seriously to be considered.

The Johnny Destiny dossier was far from closed.

"If it was him," Inspector Hood said to Dr. Morelle as the taxi bearing them Chelsea-wards turned down Gloucester Road, "he's made enough enemies. Must be plenty who had it in for him." He expelled a cloud of acrid tobacco-smoke from the side of his mouth. "But this business of the girl spotting him large as life at Southend puts a different complexion on it."

"She said that she noticed someone on the cross-channel boat who appeared to be taking an interest in him?" Dr. Morelle said.

"Just another American," Inspector Hood had said, "so he apparently told her. In fact, it looks as if it might have been someone who knew him for who he was."

"In that case," Dr. Morelle said, "one would have imagined that Destiny would in turn have recognized him and would have been on the alert. Yet according to this girl he dismissed her suggestion that he was under observation." Inspector Hood nodded. "Which may have been merely the impression he wanted to convey," Dr. Morelle said. "Not wishing to arouse her curiosity regarding himself."

"So he could have known who the other chap was all the time, and was ready for him? May have even deliberately lured him on, with the object of silencing him and then planting it to look as if he himself had been killed."

Dr. Morelle shrugged. "It is a matter for conjecture. But we know enough about Destiny to recognize that he is as resourceful as he is ruthless."

"Nothing I wouldn't put past that baby," Inspector Hood had agreed.

Following Miss Frayle's phone call to him at Scotland Yard, Inspector Hood had phoned through the information she had given him to "Spider" Bruce, before proceeding to the Judo Club in search of Dr. Morelle. And now Superintendent Bruce was welcoming them into his office, he was very much aware of the part Dr. Morelle had played in the Transatlantic business, and he had an item of news to give to Dr. Morelle and Inspector Hood, which caused the latter to clamp his teeth over his pipe-stem with a grunt that might have been of satisfaction, surprise or a mingling of both.

The fingerprint boys at Scotland Yard had been unable to find any dabs which compared with the dead man's, since Johnny Destiny wasn't filed at C.R.O. they had no prints of him to which to refer. But the prints had been radioed to Interpol in Paris, who did possess a pretty fat dossier on Johnny Destiny. They had come back promptly with the advice that the fingerprints were not his, adding the interesting information for free that in fact they belonged to an U.S. Army deserter named Cormack. Cormack had been heard of, very briefly, several months before in the vicinity of Nice. The Interpol item had come through to Chelsea only a few minutes before Dr. Morelle's and Inspector Hood's arrival.

"Seems to add up," "Spider" Bruce said to them, "this chap Cormack recognized Destiny on the boat. Maybe thought he had something on him, and tried to put the pressure on Destiny during the journey up from Folkestone, and Destiny took care of him."

"So it looks as if he's alive and over here," Inspector Hood said. "And we've got a rough idea where he might be."

"Rough is the word," "Spider" Bruce said, "but I'll get his description down to Southend, so they can keep a lookout for him."

The other nodded. "Come to think," he said with a glance at Dr. Morelle, "I wonder what he looks like now. It's a year or more since the

Transatlantic business, and a man like Johnny Destiny might change quite a bit in that time."

"Not so very much," Dr. Morelle said thoughtfully. "It would seem that he must have borne some resemblance to his passport photograph which appeared in the press, since this girl recognized him from it."

"That's true enough," Superintendent Bruce said. Inspector Hood shifted his pipe from one side of his grey moustache to the other in agreement, and the discussion quickly turned on the steps to be taken with the object of picking up Johnny Destiny, this time on a murder charge.

It was then that Dr. Morelle had expressed his concern for the safety of Erica Travers, and also Miss Frayle. The former must have made it clear to the young woman at the hoop-la stall of her suspicions regarding Johnny Destiny. If the hoop-la girl in turn had passed on this to Destiny, he would not be unaware of one quarter wherein possible danger that his impersonation might be discovered could lie.

There were, however, two aspects which made it unlikely that Erica Travers or Miss Frayle were in any imminent danger. The first as Dr. Morelle was quick to point out was that the girl at the hoop-la stall might have been telling the truth, when she had declared that Johnny Destiny was no more than a casual customer at her stall and that she was completely unaware of his identity. In which event she might never have the opportunity of acquainting Johnny Destiny with any warning information. And secondly, even if she did meet up with him again subsequently the chance that he in turn might meet up with Erica Travers or Miss Frayle seemed to be a slim one.

Nevertheless, both "Spider" Bruce and Inspector Hood were experienced enough police-officers to know that coincidence can sometimes play an extraordinarily vital part in a case, and they agreed with Dr. Morelle that it would be wise to leave nothing to chance in this matter. Erica Travers and Miss Frayle might be well advised to curtail their holiday, or remove themselves from the vicinity in which Johnny Destiny was suspected to have gone to ground.

"Another angle," Inspector Hood said, "is that if this girl at the Kursaal place does meet him again, and warns him that he's been spotted, more than likely his reaction would be to put as much distance as he can between himself and Southend in the quickest possible time."

Superintendent Bruce nodded. "You've got something there."

"Unless," Dr. Morelle said, regarding the tip of his Le Sphinx reflectively, "he has gone to that vicinity for some particular purpose." They both looked at him sharply. "He did not venture out of France merely for the pleasure of the trip, there was some lure which must have attracted him over here."

"Funny you should have said that," Inspector Hood said, scratching his heavy chin with his pipe-stem. "I was just running over in my mind that as well as Johnny Destiny who managed to give everyone the slip over the Transatlantic business, there was Danny Boy. He was English, supposing he'd decided to come home, and recently Johnny had heard about it?"

Dr. Morelle gave a faint shrug. "That might be so," he said. "Though since we don't know where this other individual is either, it doesn't help us much further regarding Destiny's present whereabouts."

"Unless they're both at Southend," "Spider" Bruce said. "Johnny Destiny went there to find him."

Inspector Hood turned a questioning gaze upon Dr. Morelle who was taking a deep drag at his Le Sphinx, but Dr. Morelle's expression remained enigmatic. "So you'll be nipping down to warn Miss Frayle and her friend, eh?" Inspector Hood said.

"Without alarming them unduly," Dr. Morelle said, "I think I might find some excuse to explain my presence in that part of the world. I shall drive down to-morrow."

Chapter Eighteen

IT WAS OBVIOUS to Miss Frayle that Aunt Edith was a character who had made quite an appeal to Dr. Morelle. The tough, open-air impression she gave was something he had not often met with in a woman, and there was no doubt he found her complete absence of femininity a refreshing change.

After Miss Frayle's encounter with Dr. Morelle and he had helped her climb out of the water onto the jetty, she had introduced Erica and Jim Rayner to the unexpected visitor. She had hurried off to the *Moya* to change into a frock and fix her hair which she felt convinced gave her the appearance of a drowned rat, leaving Jim to return to the yacht, while Erica had brought Dr. Morelle aboard the houseboat.

When Miss Frayle had reappeared she found Dr. Morelle being shown over the *Moya* by Aunt Edith, smoking one of her cheroots, and he was apparently fairly interested in what he saw. Lunch in the saloon had followed, with Dr. Morelle silent as he listened to Aunt Edith holding forth in her inimitable style upon the *Moya* and her passion for ornithology, which compelled her to spend so much time aboard her beloved vessel.

Dr. Morelle had given as his explanation for his arrival out of the blue that he had planned to visit a certain Professor Stenberg, who lived at Lower Ashton, a small place on the other side of Sharbridge. Dr. Morelle and the professor had been colleagues in London, before the latter had retired to devote himself entirely to research. Dr. Morelle made his explanation sound most convincing to his listeners, except Miss Frayle, who felt pretty certain it was something quite different which had brought him so unexpectedly to this part of the world.

It was not until Aunt Edith was in the galley, having insisted on washing-up, that Miss Frayle and Erica Travers found themselves giving Dr. Morelle a detailed account of what had occurred at Southend Kursaal, and Miss Frayle sensed what it was that lay behind Dr. Morelle's appearance on the scene. Erica told her story again from the beginning, how she had met the man on the cross-channel steamer, although she had not known his name was Johnny Destiny until she had read it in the newspaper. She had recalled the apparent unconcern with which he had reacted to her observation that another man was watching him.

This other man, she had told Dr. Morelle, was similar in build to Destiny, and might well have been, as he had suggested he was, another American. She explained how she had thought no more about the episode until she had seen the photograph and read the newspaper report of the discovery of his body in the boat-train at Victoria. Here, Miss Frayle had added her account of how she had not considered Erica's story as she had told it to her at the time of any significance. And then that sudden recognition of Johnny Destiny at the Kursaal. That extraordinary coincidence had appeared significant enough and Miss Frayle, failing to contact Dr. Morelle, had got in touch with Inspector Hood.

"And you felt convinced that this girl at the hoop-la stall was lying, when she denied that she was unaware of his identity?" Dr. Morelle had said to Erica.

"It was the way she got annoyed with me," Erica said. "That's what made me think she knew him all right."

Dr. Morelle regarded her speculatively through a cloud of cigarette smoke. He was considering what possible danger she had brought upon herself as a result of impetuously involving herself in this business. So much better if she and Miss Frayle had remained in the background, quietly observing what had transpired and then passed on the result of what they had noted to the proper authorities. It seemed apparent to him that Miss Frayle had tried to curb the other's eagerness to play the amateur detective, but had failed.

He gave no hint of what was in his mind: of the conclusions he and Inspector Hood, together with the railway-detective and the detective-superintendent of B Division, had arrived at during their conference yesterday afternoon. He made no reference to the phone call he had received from Inspector Hood that morning before he had left 221b Harley Street, to the effect that the Southend police had checked at the Kursaal: they had found the girl at the hoop-la stall who was in the absent Lucilla's place and deciding that she was bright and sensible, had taken her into their confidence to an extent sufficient for their purpose, and elicited from her a description of the individual with whom Lucilla had gone off with to spend yesterday evening.

The police had also learned that the girl known as Lucilla would not be returning to the Kursaal for a day or two. Where had she gone? The other girl didn't know. Nor had the police so far discovered Lucilla's address in Southend. Their inquiries in that direction had come to a temporary dead end.

But what could now be counted as certain was that Johnny Destiny knew he had been recognized at the Kursaal.

"It is most likely," Dr. Morelle had said to Erica Travers, "that when he learns from this girl you were questioning her about him, he will decide to quit the vicinity forthwith. Until that seems established, however," and he paused momentarily, contemplating the tip of his Le Sphinx, "then you had both better restrain your enthusiasm for sampling the allure and delights of Southend."

Erica's face showed a suitably apprehensive flicker. "Point taken," she said. "In that case, I'm staying put." She glanced at Miss Frayle, who smiled at her in a manner that was meant to convey approval mingled with a not-to-worry-unduly expression.

"So long as Dr. Morelle's here," Miss Frayle said, "everything will be all right."

It was at that moment that Aunt Edith had chosen to return to the saloon, striding in, her spirits as buoyant as a cork on water. She caught the slight tension in the air, and her hearty manner softened as she listened to what Erica had to tell her. "You think it may be quite a serious business?" she said, turning to Dr. Morelle.

"She could possibly run into danger if this man encountered her again," he said quietly.

"I see," Aunt Edith stroked her strong chin pensively, and looked at her niece. "Must admit I thought it was all a lot of imagination on your part. What do you advise, Dr. Morelle?"

"Nothing, except keep out of the way. The whole business will soon be cleared up."

"I certainly hope so," Aunt Edith said.

Erica flashed her a reassuring smile. "I shan't stray far from here until it is," she said.

"So perhaps you'll be able to cope with an odd job or two around here," Aunt Edith said promptly, and Erica laughed. "In between your sunbathing, of course. One you can start in on right away. Up on deck."

"Not polishing the brasswork?" Erica said, with a groan, and while Aunt Edith indicated to her that it was a simple and not especially tiresome matter of some new porthole curtains, for which the material and all the measurements were prepared, Erica looked at Miss Frayle. "Why don't you show Dr. Morelle around?"

"The breeze is freshening," Aunt Edith had said, chiming in vigorously. "Ideal for a look-round; if you don't know these parts, Dr. Morelle, here's your chance. Got everything except mountains, we have. Whether your interest is marine biology, ornithology or even archaeology, there's enough to keep you occupied. The earthworks and keep over at Thallerton. The old ruins of Pebcreek Church, which isn't more than half a mile by the footpath."

And that was how Miss Frayle now came to be giving Dr. Morelle an account of what she considered was the eerie incident of the limping man in the churchyard, as they made their way along the footpath in the direction of old Pebcreek Church. Miss Frayle had leapt at the opportunity put up all unwittingly by Aunt Edith of satisfying her somewhat morbid curiosity which had clung so tenaciously to the back of her mind, by revisiting the scene of the strange occurrence in the company of Dr. Morelle, of all people.

"He acted so strangely," Miss Frayle said. "Turning away just as if he didn't want to be seen, and disappearing." Dr. Morelle permitted himself one of his bleak smiles, but she wasn't to be dampened. The footpath was still soggy from the storm two days before, but she continued on, Dr. Morelle keeping pace with her indulgently, his eyes taking in the sun-drenched, yet oddly desolate beauty of the scene, his mind preoccupied with the possibilities which might be opened up by this intriguing arrival in the vicinity of Johnny Destiny.

They neared the trees on the crown of the low hill, the path almost losing its identity in bracken and spreading creeper, reminding Miss Frayle of the grave-strewn wilderness on the further side of the church. She related to Dr. Morelle the tragic story that Erica had told her. How the old village of Pebcreek had been flooded and the consequent neglect of the church, its gradual decay over the years to its present ruin.

Miss Frayle recalled how Jim Rayner had mentioned that the place was reputed to be haunted. At this, as she had expected Dr. Morelle's saturnine features appeared even more sardonic in expression. He made the comment that it was to be expected that after a catastrophe such stories were inevitable; he wondered if the disaster to the old village had been exaggerated over the years on that account.

But Miss Frayle wasn't listening to him. Fact or legend, haunted or not, she was experiencing once more the eerie, oppressive atmosphere as soon as they gained the shadows of the trees; the same feeling that had assailed her in the graveyard. Then, of course, there had been the thunderstorm to heighten the malevolent effect. Now, the sun was shining, though it failed to penetrate the thick leafy trees. It was light enough, but greenish-hued, deep shadows spread everywhere, the only sounds the occasional snapping of a dead twig underfoot and the flapping wings of a silent bird.

Miss Frayle stopped suddenly, to point out the crumbling stonework of the church just discernible through the trees ahead. Dr. Morelle's glance flickered over the path of crumpled ferns leading to the church. He turned to Miss Frayle mockingly. "What next?" he said.

She bit her lip with aggravation, he might at least humour her by pretending to appear impressed. They moved on, Miss Frayle was finding herself keeping close behind him. There was the crumbling vestry, and even as she stood still to regard the door which was closed, she saw the shrubs and nettles around it had been trampled down. Dr. Morelle appeared not to discern any significance in the sight as he pulled at the broken door-handle. The door creaked outwards.

"You first," Miss Frayle said, trying to get a light note into her voice.

Dr. Morelle stepped inside. The atmosphere struck chill and damp on their faces. The gloom was suddenly illuminated by a flickering halo of light from Dr. Morelle's cigarette-lighter. He went forward, Miss Frayle practically treading on his heels. "Steps go down under the church, probably to the crypt," he said. He spoke quietly, yet his voice had a strange echoing sound.

Silently Miss Frayle followed him slowly down the worn steps. The movement of the tiny flame cast grotesque dancing shadows on the white chipped walls. The air became chillier and stale, with the damp smell of moss in their nostrils. The steps turned sharply and opened out into a small space. A faint gleam of daylight seeped through to the flagstoned walls. Miss Frayle noticed that it came through a hole in the ceiling, this proved to be the end of a crude ventilator-shaft, and when she stood beneath it she could see a small grid covering the opening at ground level.

"I should estimate this to be directly under the church," Dr. Morelle was saying, glancing up. His voice was low yet in the confined space it sounded boomingly in Miss Frayle's ear. He held the flame of his lighter up close to the opening. "It has been excavated recently."

"By the man I saw?" Miss Frayle spoke in a tiny whisper.

Dr. Morelle was remembering the trampled-down path through the grass and weeds to the vestry-door. He shrugged non-committally. "This was once probably a private vault," he said. "It isn't large enough for anything else. An old tomb there." He indicated a long coffin-shaped slab of stone and was rewarded by a shudder from Miss Frayle.

"I think we ought to go," she said, nervously.

But Dr. Morelle had moved to the coffin-like stone and was applying the flame of his lighter to a small oil-lamp he had seen. He broke off and said: "This lamp is still warm." Miss Frayle gave a start as he held up the lamp, now lit.

In its light there was a table against one wall, and nearby stood something covered by layers of sacking. Dr. Morelle gave it his attention for a few moments. Miss Frayle gazed at him over her horn-rims. His gaunt features seemed carved from ivory in the flickering light, his eyes dark, sombre and narrowed beneath his black, craggy eyebrows. A wisp of smoke curled from his cigarette as he moved in and pulled the sacking away to reveal something that glinted dully.

"Machinery?" Miss Frayle said wide-eyed. Dr. Morelle was staring down reflectively. Miss Frayle drew in her breath. "It looks like a printing-press."

"Precisely, Miss Frayle," Dr. Morelle said.

Chapter Nineteen

EVEN THOUGH THE afternoon sun was warm, the terrain appeared to him bleak, uninviting. He thought it was a good place to bury yourself; and he supposed it couldn't be better for what was hatching out in the darkness of his mind.

"This is Pebcreek," the girl beside him said. "This is the village."

All that took his attention was the police-station, which brought a faint grin to his face. He made with the chat about the scene and drove along the street. It was not like driving the Merc. The car he'd hired was an old model, a popular make. He didn't want a flashy heap anyway. Not this time. Something ordinary that wouldn't attract too much notice in this backwater of a place.

"Follow the road, along by the river."

He nodded and put his foot down when they cleared the village. The road was too snaky, the surface too poor for any speed. He sat silent at the wheel as the car rattled along, the smile on his face covering the thoughts behind his pale eyes. He was looking forward to the end of the trip. He'd come a long way. He thought it was going to be worth it.

He wasn't so sure of the sort of welcome that awaited him, but so what? He figured he held all the cards. So if the guy had changed, if he had settled down to scratch a living from a seedy waterside pub? There were still links with the past.

The car dropped down from a shallow hill towards a hump-backed bridge and he eased his foot off the accelerator. He could see a creek twisting in from the river, but as they descended the water was hidden from them by a high river wall. Ahead, where the wall levelled out with the road he saw a brick and boarded building of low, rambling shape. His glance shifted momentarily beyond and took in the jetty, a moored boat, a car nearby, a cottage opposite, across the road. It was pretty much the way he expected and it suited him okay. He glanced at the girl beside him.

"This is it," she said. "This is all there is of Dormouse Creek."

"You like it, don't you?" He took his hand off the wheel to fondle her hair above the nape of her neck. "I guess it kind of grows on you."

"Yes," she said quietly. "I never thought Dad would settled down here, but he has. Gossips with the locals in the bar, or wanders the marsh with his gun. The living's not much but he's never been so happy."

He nodded, his gaze narrowed a little, taking the scene in. "It's got something. Sort of draws you, land and water all mixed up like this." He was looking at the inn, with its sign sticking out, weather-beaten and faded. He couldn't see how anyone could stick it when they'd known the gilt and plush, easy living.

The girl's dark, lustrous eyes were shining with anticipation. "It's a nice surprise for him," she said.

"A very nice surprise," he said to her.

He turned the car off the road and, following her directions, drove through a gate between a shed and a lean-to outbuilding that formed one end of the house. He stopped the car in the yard and got out.

He could see the back of the place. It was brickwork so far as the ground-floor window-sills; the rest of it was built of wood. Long, black overlapping boards. At some time in the distant past, the house had been given an extension. One part of the roof was higher than the other. The older portion was roofed with tiles, the addition was slate. The tiles were breaking away and so was part of the gutter. It drooped down at the end waiting for the next high wind. The drain-pipes were rusty at the joints, they emptied into two round water-butts, one close to the backdoor, the other at the far corner of the house. There weren't many windows at the back, just three on the ground floor and two up. The glass looked smeared, as if recent rains had the salt of the marshes in them and had left it on the windows.

He followed the girl to a narrow wooden porch. He had a glimpse of flower-beds and shrubs and beyond, fruit-trees. She rattled the latch of the back door and eventually the catch was released. They went into a low, dark scullery. A low, grubby sink with a pump over it beneath the small window. A massive copper jutting out from the wall opposite. Round the walls shelves of old bottles, some with candle-ends in them. An old dresser lined one wall with a load of junk on it. Oil-lamps, cans, a reel of string and paper cluttered its top and shelves. There was nothing else in the scullery. Nothing, he thought, but spiders and flies. It wasn't so much that it was dirty, it was just the sort of place that would never look clean. It stank of poverty.

The kitchen looked better. The windows were larger and one of them was open. The wallpaper had faded, but it was still a light colour. There wasn't much furniture. But it had been kept dusted and polished. There was a table in the centre with a swinging oil-lamp above.

A heavy silence hung on the musty, dampish atmosphere.

"He's certainly not expecting you," he said.

She was frowning. She crossed to the open window, looking out. She turned to him again. She came back across the room to the door, to call out into the passage. There was no reply. "I think I know where he is," she said. "Stick around, I'll get him."

"Where'll he be?"

"Not far," her tone was suddenly evasive.

"Shall I come with you?"

She shook her head and started to move down the passage towards the scullery, but he caught her by the shoulders.

"Give me something to think over, hon, while I'm waiting." He took her in his arms and kissed her lingeringly. Breathless, she drew away, turned and went out. He grinned after her thinly. He took a packet of cigarettes out of his pocket, tapped a cigarette from it and his gold Cartier lighter flamed into life. He began to pad along the passage to the stairs. From there he could look into the bar. Over the doorway was a stuffed wild-fowl in a glass case. The floor of the room was just rough boards. Oil-lamps in wall-brackets and the plain varnished paper was smoke-stained. A dart board opposite the outside door, the wall all around it pitted with dart-marks. A couple of sporting-prints on the other wall. Some hard-backed chairs, and wooden benches with deal tables in front of them. The bar itself was little more than a trap in the wall which divided the room from the passage. Just opposite this past the stairs, was a recess with a stand fitted to the wall on which were bottles and glasses, and shelves behind equipped with earthenware and pewter mugs.

Dragging at his cigarette he went down the passage as far as the bar and just beyond it saw the curtained archway leading down a couple of steps into the cellar. He could see the beer-kegs and crates of bottles, but there wasn't a big stock. The other side of the cellar entrance was a wall showcase, its shelves sparsely furnished with tobacco and packets of cigarettes. A door opposite with a lifting glass shutter opened into a small room furnished with tables, a long sofa and black-hide chairs. He could just make out the inscription on the outside door: BAR PARLOUR.

Two other rooms on the ground floor; but they were no more than half-furnished and had the appearance of never having been lived in.

He paused listening for voices that meant the girl's and her father's return. He slipped quietly upstairs. The landing was long and gloomy, paint and paper dark, dull with age. Four bedrooms and a smaller room with a stained, enamel bath in it. There were no taps. A huge enamel jug stood in a china bowl on the washstand, and like the bedrooms, the sloping floor was covered with cheap linoleum and thin mats.

One of the larger bedroom's was obviously the man's; it was untidy, the bed still unmade, an air of shiftlessness about it, as if its occupant had no intention of staying any length of time. He went out of the room and down the stairs. The whole place had a dingy, poverty-stricken atmosphere which gave him the creeps.

It was very quiet in the kitchen. The stillness was disturbed now and then by the distant call of a marshland bird seeping into the room. He glanced at his watch. It said a couple of minutes past three o'clock. He noticed that the clock on the wall had gone haywire, it was ticking away like crazy, but the time it gave was five minutes past twelve. He glanced at his watch again. He supposed it explained why the dump was so quiet. So still. It was shut up till opening-time again in the evening. Not that it looked as if it did a roaring trade even when it was open, at that. But the girl had explained how it didn't bother her old man that he wasn't rushed off his feet with customers.

The sudden movement behind his back brought him pivoting round on his heel, his right hand instinctively starting to reach up to the left side of his jacket. Then he relaxed, he lowered his hand again slowly and his face creased in a smile at the man who stood there.

He had come in through the door that led to the scullery and outside, the way the girl had gone. His face was sunburnt, but there was the same old greyish tinge beneath the tan. His hair was thin and brushed back from a bony forehead. He looked as if he hadn't changed a bit, the other man thought. He was wearing a nondescript suit with an open-necked shirt, above the collar of which his Adam's apple worked convulsively, his eyes were protruding out of their sockets, as if he was staring at a ghost.

"Hello, there," Johnny Destiny said, making it sound casual, though his voice rasped a little, and without taking the cigarette out of his mouth.

And he moved easily forward and held out his hand to Danny Boy.

Chapter Twenty

DANNY BOY RECOVERED himself quickly. After that first shock Johnny could see the way he pulled himself together sufficiently to say: "You staying long?"

Johnny's grin broadened. This was how he'd figured it would go. This was how he'd hoped the other would take it. This was the way it had to go. He felt expansive now as his pale glance flickered over the familiar figure before him. He knew now he'd played it right with the daughter. The way he had figured it that she'd had only a hazy idea of her fathers' racket; if she'd been suspicious at all that it hadn't been quite on the level, he was sure she didn't know just how far off-track he had been. Like she could know he'd deserted from the British forces in Italy. She could know that. But she wouldn't know a thing about the Transatlantic caper. He felt sure of that. She wouldn't know he was wanted by the gendarmes. He hadn't given the show away and disillusioned her about her old man. Apart from it not getting him any place, it would have antagonized Danny. No point in kicking off on the wrong foot, even if he had to get tough later. And maybe he wouldn't have to get so tough. But that was up to Danny.

He let his gaze wander around the kitchen.

"Depends," he said lightly. "You got it nice here. I like these parts. I could use a vacation." He could read Danny's mind from the expression on his face. He knew Danny must have read it in the newspapers about him having been done in on the boat train. He smiled to himself at that. Then he tried to figure it out how Danny had taken it. But anyway his arrival like this must have given him one hell of a shock. He really must have thought he was seeing a ghost.

Again he had to hand it to Danny the way he had reacted.

Danny gave a short laugh.

"Not much in the way of entertainment here," he said. "It's the world's end. Not like — like Rome, for instance."

"I can take Rome, or leave it alone," Johnny said. "Like I told Lucilla, I go for the simple things."

The other's eyes slitted. Johnny had been expecting Lucilla to show with her father, and was beginning to wonder where she'd got to, now he realized that she hadn't found him and brought Danny along to meet him. She was still looking for her father.

"She brought you?" Danny looked baffled.

"She was going to introduce us," Johnny said, without smiling. He knew at once that this was the tricky part. Dragging his kid into it, Danny might take a poor view of that.

"I never guessed you knew each other." Danny turned away, he began whistling under his breath and Johnny's face unfroze. He watched the other cracking the knuckles of his spatulate fingers, and it made him feel that it was just like old times. It was going to be even more like old times before the world had taken many more whirls. "When the papers said you were dead," Danny said, and turned back to him, "it came as a bit of a shock."

"I can imagine," Johnny said smoothly. "It was just a little gimmick to ensure I'd left no trail behind." His lips curled back wolfishly. "This other character, I forget who he was, and it doesn't matter a damn, he had the same gag in mind. He'd spotted me on the boat coming over. He must have remembered me from way back somewhere, though I never remembered him. When he tried to do for me, just like that," Johnny's tone sounded quite aggrieved, "I saw him coming, and got mine in first. He'd given me an idea, so I did to him what I figured he aimed to do to me." He lit a fresh cigarette and it drooped from the corner of his mouth. "I bashed him around with his own Luger so his own mother wouldn't have known him. The rest was simple. It paid off, too. Well, I thought, I'd be a fool to pass up an opportunity like that."

Danny nodded slowly. "You always were pretty quick on the up-take," he said. "Like that time in Brussels, remember? So when I read you'd cashed in your chips, I didn't break my heart over it."

"Take it easy," Johnny said. "I didn't do dirt on you in Brussels, you know that. It was the Lizard mob who double-crossed both of us. I saw you picked up, but how would I have helped by butting in?"

Danny shrugged as if it couldn't matter less. "You didn't tell Lucilla who you were, or anything?"

"No," Johnny said, "I gave her the label I'm travelling under these days. Same as I didn't query the name you're using." He saw the other's tension slacken, and again he congratulated himself for playing it the way he had.

"So you found out where she was?" Danny said.

"I remembered you talking about her once or twice; then that photo you had of her. It just stuck in the back of my mind, you know, the way things do." Danny didn't say anything, the kitchen was very silent except for the ticking clock on the wall, and Johnny could hear his own voice as if he was listening to someone else talking.

"Then I happened to pick up an item of news over the grapevine in Vichy, that you were well under wraps somewhere in this part of the world, and that the kid was working the carney at the place you call Southend. So I thought, why shouldn't I look you up? And here little Johnny is, dropped in for a cosy chin about old times."

"You found Lucilla at the Kursaal, and she fell for your smooth gab?"

"You know how it is with me and the dames." The other spread his hands in a helpless gesture. "She's a sweet kid, let me tell you that. Real sweet. You should be real proud of her."

Danny glanced round as if he was expecting the girl to put in an appearance. Johnny explained how she'd gone in search of him. Danny said something about they must have managed to miss each other, though he hadn't been so far away. The pub hadn't long closed for the afternoon, customers wouldn't be dropping in until evening, though they didn't usually look in at the Wildfowler until late evening this time of the year.

If he hadn't sensed it, Johnny could hear it in his voice that behind the façade he had thrown up, Danny was definitely shaken by his reappearance in his life.

"Danny," Johnny said softly, without taking his cigarette out of his mouth. "She don't need to know a thing. Not the way I figure it."

"I don't want to hear the way you figure it," Danny said, and Johnny saw that suddenly his hands were trembling. "All I want is you should leave me out of it."

"Not before you're heard what I've come to say." Johnny took his cigarette from between his thin lips and very slowly blew a spiral of smoke ceilingwards. "I've come a long way to say it. Relax, Danny, and listen to what's on my mind."

He jerked his head round and stood listening. Danny watched him, then he crossed to the door to the scullery which stood ajar and he pushed it wider. He came back into the room, shaking his head. "Sounded like it was someone," Johnny said.

"Place is full of noises. It was nothing. But, listen Johnny, the kid'll be back any minute. She doesn't know about me. She may have a suspicion I wasn't on the level during the war and afterwards. But she thinks I've levelled out for good. I want her to keep thinking that way."

Johnny glanced round and let his expression tell the other what he thought of what he saw.

"Don't kid yourself, Danny. You wouldn't want to pass up this opportunity, when I've drawn the maps for you. Look, I'll take care of everything. Sure, I don't aim to take you away from this. You want it should be this way. All I aim is you should be more comfortable here. You haven't lost your old touch. Why, the mere thought of it sometimes must make your fingers itch. Don't you see, you and me in the perfect set-up. This place as our H.Q. Miles from anywhere. In a few months we'd make enough to live on for the rest of our fives. I'd clear off. Back to the States, South America, wherever. Danny, we can't miss."

"Nothing doing, Johnny," Danny said quietly. "I'm finished with the racket."

"Don't give me that, I bet you could set up operations at the drop of a hat. I bet you got some caper up your sleeve all the time, all you want is someone like me to spark it." He was half-kidding him, he felt convinced that what the other had said he meant, and that he'd have to work on him quite a while. "Why, I bet you even got a plant ready to go to work for you, some place." He gave a look around as if suggesting that Danny had a hiding-place on the premises. "You never give up a love like that." It was then that he could have sworn he saw the muscles in Danny's hand tighten, and he wondered if for all that he'd only been kidding, he'd hit the spot. Maybe Danny had got ideas, maybe he had got a press stashed away against a time when he could get to work again.

Danny was shaking his head slowly. "Even if it wasn't for the kid," he said, "I'm staying out."

Johnny flicked his cigarette-stub into the empty grate. His mouth was a hard, tight fine. He had a hunch that Danny was lying to him. He felt it in the air that he had a caper set up for himself.

"Your final word, Danny?" His lips hardly moved.

Danny came over to him. He stood there, nondescript and older-looking now than Rome, and Johnny knew that there was still magic yet in those fingers. "No hard feelings," Danny said, and he sounded as if his heart was in his words. "But you go your way and leave me to stay put. I don't never want any part of it again. Never. So on your way, Johnny, and good luck go with you."

"Before I go maybe you should hear my final word." He drew in his breath between his teeth. To Danny it sounded like a snake when about to strike. "So you think I'm going to pass it up just on account of you not wanting to play ball? It ain't natural. So how do you leave me? So I'll tell you. So I got to resort to a little persuasion, to put my side of it to you. If you see what I mean."

He pulled out the packet of cigarettes, tapped out one and with an affable grin offered the packet to Danny, who shook his head. Johnny took a cigarette for himself and with studied casualness pushed the packet back into his pocket. He caught the other's glance fasten on his lighter. The look in Danny's eyes didn't tell him very much, as he lit his cigarette and took a long drag at it.

"You got Lucilla to think of, like you said," Johnny said. "But I sympathize with you. She's sweet, real sweet. You wouldn't want her to see you wind up in the cooler. Just on account of some sneaking rat went and tipped off the gendarmes about her old man." The other made a movement, and Johnny grinned, spreading his hands. "You see how it is with me Danny? I'm really serious."

The other had moved closer, the greyness of his face showing pale now beneath the sun-tan, and he was about to say something, when light footsteps sounded from the scullery and the door opened, Lucilla stood on the threshold, her dark gaze on her father.

"So there you are," she said.

"Hello," Danny said, and once again Johnny had to hand it to him for the way he forced his tone to hide the feelings that his words must have aroused in him. "I'm sorry you had to go looking for me, I wasn't a mile away."

"I gave you a yell, but there was no reply," she said. "Anyway, you've already introduced yourselves." She looked at Johnny as if she was hoping they'd hit it off together. "He's an American," she said. "We met in Southend, but perhaps you've discovered all about that." She laughed. "He's very nice, and he wants to stay here for a night or two. You can give him a room, can't you?"

She glanced at Danny, then back to Johnny again, her eyes bright with affection.

"Sure," Johnny said, "your pop and I soon got acquainted. I told him how I'd taken a fancy to this neck of the woods, isn't that right?" He turned to Danny, whose hands were hanging at his sides, the fingers clenching and unclenching again. "Your pop's real kind, too, he says sure I can rest my weary head for a couple of nights."

"That's fine," Lucilla said, she seemed to be brimming over with happiness as she moved to her father and took his arm. Danny and Johnny stared at each other silently, the former thinking what to say as the girl chatted on, and in answer to the mocking glint in Johnny's gaze, masked by a cloud of cigarette-smoke.

Although she stood close to him, Danny didn't realize that Lucilla's legs were trembling, that her blood was running cold, that she was seeing her father and Johnny through a mist of horrified shock.

Neither of them guessed that she had been outside the door all the time, that she'd heard every word that her father and Johnny had said.

Chapter Twenty-One

HE STRETCHED HIMSELF out on the bed. It wasn't all that soft, but he'd slept on worse. Slept on better, too. And by hell, he would sleep on better beds yet before he was through.

The sounds of the inn-yard came up to him through the open window, a rooster crowed, a hen clucked, a dog barked in the distance. From somewhere came the croak of some wild bird. He lay there relaxed, that thin smile creeping across his face, that smile of complacency, as he told himself it was all sewn up.

He turned the pages of the paper-backed book he was reading, about guns. It was an American book he'd picked up in Nice a while back. He was interested in guns. He read in a chapter which was devoted to handguns how a .22 pistol loaded with high-speed hollow-point ammunition was no toy, but that unless a man was hit in a specially vulnerable spot, such as between the eyes, a .22 bullet wouldn't stop him. Not fast enough for safety. A man could have received a mortal wound but could still shoot back. The lightest cartridge that can be depended on to stop a man was the .38 special.

He read on about the comparisons between revolvers and automatic-pistols. The Colt .45 Army semi-automatic pistol, he read, was a powerful gun, generally rated the best military semi-automatic pistol. However, even it was no more reliable than the ammunition it fired, if it misfires, the gun stops. Both hands, and time, would be needed to clear the jammed gun. If on the other hand, a revolver misfires it could go on shooting. The cylinder rolls a fresh cartridge into place regardless of whether the previous cartridge fired or not.

Revolvers, the book said, of .38 calibre or larger are easier to shoot than semi-automatic pistols of similar power. They possessed better trigger pulls. Furthermore unless the pistol was not only loaded but cocked, which was highly dangerous and asking for trouble, it was slower with the first shot than a double-action revolver. He nodded his head to himself and reflected that the larger calibre semi-automatic pistol is okay only in skilled hands, and most who know how to shoot it prefer a revolver, which was why he preferred a revolver.

He went on to read how both Colt, and Smith and Wesson made a wide variety of revolvers. The target-revolver, the K 38 Smith and Wesson, for example, with its modern short action and broad hammer spur. But this gun had a six-inch barrel, it was a little large to keep in a bedside drawer.

Both Colt, and Smith and Wesson, he knew, made guns with shorter barrels. He remembered the standard police revolver he'd once had, before he'd come East, a four-inch barrel with fixed sights, chambered for a .38 special cartridge. A gun with a longer barrel wouldn't be so easily and quickly drawn from a holster. The fixed sights were all right, too. Then he'd once owned a Smith and Wesson combat model, which had a Baughman front sight, rounded so it wouldn't catch in the holster, an open-front holster made by J. H. Martin of Calhoun City, Mississippi, and known as the Berns-Martin. It held the gun with a spring-clasp. In drawing the gun you didn't have to lift it out of the holster, you simply pushed it forward and down.

He lit himself another cigarette and dragged at it for a while, thinking of the man in the boat-train railway-compartment. The funny, surprised look when he'd shot him clean between the eyes. Just like it said you should stop a man in the book. He began reading some more. Shooting for keeps, he read, requires far less precision. But it does require practice. You may have to shoot in the dark, you may have to shoot fast. You point the gun at waist level and shoot. Shooting from waist height, means you must depend on pointing the gun as you might point your finger.

He read that you should grip a revolver as if you liked it. Your grasp should be high on the gun and firm. The grip of his Colt Detective Special was made small, so the gun was compact. He couldn't find room for his little finger, so he curled it under the butt. Shooting the .38 special cartridge made it jump a bit and it had a loud bark, owing to the short barrel. Neither the jump nor the bark ever hurt anyone.

He swung his legs off the bed and stood up. He smoothed his silk shirt and crossed to the dressing-table. Expertly he strapped the Detective Special in the holster under his left arm-pit. He wasn't left-handed.

He put on his jacket and glanced at his watch. It was pushing seven o'clock. He went downstairs. He thought he'd never had it so good.

Lucilla found him lounging back on a chair in the kitchen, relaxed, a cigarette drooping from his lips and a half-empty whisky glass in his hand.

He pulled her down to him and kissed her, and she made her kisses as warm and lingering.

After the big act she had put up she had continued to keep mostly out of his way. She had said nothing of what she had overheard to her father on the few occasions she had seen him alone.

She had given the impression to them both that she took it for granted Johnny was staying, and had busied herself getting one of the bedrooms ready. Johnny had gone out to the car for his suitcase and later, when he had unpacked and gone downstairs, she had taken the opportunity to creep back to take a look at his room. Her heart racing she had glimpsed through the drawers in the dressing-table. But the few belongings he had brought along had told her nothing.

At the same time she had been alert, listening, observing Johnny and her father, watching for any sign that hinted that there was going to be another scene between them, like the one she had overheard a few hours earlier. But there was no sign, Johnny behaved with his usual relaxed charm, and there was little to indicate what her father was thinking. He was a little quieter perhaps, but that was the only difference.

She wondered anxiously if he was in fact seriously considering Johnny's proposition. Perhaps, she thought, he had given her father time to think it over. Maybe that was what her father was doing. A few more hours of Johnny around, another threatening scene when she was out of the way, and her father might give in; accept Johnny's blackmailing terms.

She heard her father's voice in the bar-parlour. He was gossiping with one of the customers. She wondered what he was really thinking, what agonies of anxiety and apprehension now filled his mind. She had known about the glinting machine hidden under the sacking underneath the old church for a long time. She had spotted her father going to the place one night and without realizing the significance of his surreptitious errand she had followed him. Intrigued, but scared that what she had done might arouse his anger, she had not made her presence known. After he had left, she had taken a look around.

She couldn't guess what the machinery was in aid of. But the mere fact that her father had secreted it in this isolated place, where the chance of it being discovered was negligible, and that he had not confided in her about it, was sufficient. She had always sensed that there was something in his past that was sinister and which he was trying to live down, to forget. She had felt sure that this strange hide-out she had stumbled on held some dark secret from the old days. Something to do with his travels abroad, after the war. Something which was crooked.

As Johnny's hands caressed her, and she held him in the sort of embrace she knew he was expecting of her she felt the sinister bulge under his arm. She felt him tense and shift his position, so that her arms no longer held him in the same way. He didn't say anything. Nor did she.

The shock of learning that he was a criminal, a murderer, that he'd killed the man on the train, had faded a little. She was no longer hearing his voice, cold, inhuman so that she'd barely recognized it. She would have sworn it was a stranger if she hadn't known it was her father and Johnny there. The suffocating feeling that it was all a terrible nightmare had left her.

Whatever her father may have done, she had told herself always, it was past and done with. She had helped him begin afresh. She'd imagined that it wasn't easy for him to break with the mode of life he'd led, that he still hankered after his old ways. Even to the extent of making the old crypt in the ruined church into some sort of secret workshop. One day, she had promised herself, she would tackle him about it. And if it was something sinister, to do with his shadowy past, she would make him promise to destroy the lot. Dump it all into the river.

And now this man who was Johnny Destiny, though he called himself by another name, had to come on the scene. He had to fool her into leading him back to her father. She understood now. He had used her to that end, everything he'd told her, his interest in her background, where she lived, had all been part of the crafty plot he'd weaved to fasten on her father again.

It was not so much her own feelings, as the danger she had brought upon herself and her father by bringing this man to The Wildfowler. This ruthless murderer from the past who had come to threaten, to blackmail her father into working with him again. She recalled somebody at the Kursaal saying something they'd read in the papers about the death of a man on a train at Victoria.

Johnny Destiny had killed him and left his body with battered head to appear as if it was himself. "*I saw him coming and got mine in first. I bashed him around with his own Luger so his own mother wouldn't have known him.*" Destiny had killed a man and planted on the victim his own identity. His motive, to destroy any trail he may have left; to ensure he could continue his life of crime, safe in the knowledge that the world thought him dead.

And drag her father into the abyss with him.

"Drink up, Johnny," she said, holding out her hand for his glass.

"Sure, hon."

He kept his eyes on her as he knocked back the remainder of the drink. They followed her when she went across the room. She went and got him a large whisky. She gave herself a gin. She drowned the gin in tonic water.

When she had come back he had the drink in his hand; she raised her own glass.

"Here's to us, Johnny," she said.

"Just you and me, hon," he said.

She leaned back in a chair and crossed her legs, smiling at him. His eyes focussed on her legs, and then moved upward until he was looking into her face. He crooked a finger at her.

"Come and sit close to me, hon," he said. "I been missing you."

"You sound like you really mean it, Johnny, darling," she swept a dark curl of hair over the flimsy collar of her loosely-fitting shirt and the movement exposed a creamy shoulder. "Wonder if your miss is as great as mine?"

He took another gulp from his glass and studied her again.

"You're beautiful," he said.

"I'm stifled." She laughed at him, her eyes very bright. "It's so warm in here." She threw a glance at the window. "It's lovely outside."

"So let's go see." Johnny got to his feet. He crossed to her and let his hand stroke her hair and come to rest on her bare shoulder. "You going to take me for a walk?"

She took his hand and squeezing it teasingly pressed it against her cheek.

"I've got a favourite spot not far from here," she said. "Out by the creek."

Johnny lifted her up gently until she was standing beside him.

"That I have to see, hon," he said.

They went out through the back way, she led him across a patch of spiky grass up on to the river wall, following the creek towards the river. The evening was warm, the ripple of the tide a faint whisper seeping across the mud-flats. A distant white haze was beginning to drape the river and marsh, it would become a curtain of muslin in the moonlight.

Behind them a pair of eyes, speculative in the greyish face with the hair thinning over the bony forehead, watched them until they were out of sight. But if they had been oblivious that their departure from The Wildfowler had not been entirely unobserved, neither had for a moment suspected that they had come into the range of vision of someone else who had caught them and held them sufficiently long enough in the lens of a pair of powerful field-glasses.

Johnny glanced at the dark, sultry-looking girl beside him, as if he sensed her anticipation. She led him down off the wall on to a grassy plateau that fringed the high-water mark. This was formed by the wall curving sharply into the marshland and then out again into the creek. The patch of grassland inside stretched to the edge of the tideline where reeds and sedge-grass flourished.

When they got down they were hidden by the river wall at their back and on two sides, and in front by the wild grasses lining the inlet. Except for one end where a narrow sandspit ran out. Lucilla led Johnny towards this. He sank down on to the grass but before he could pull her down beside him, she kicked off her shoes and stepped across to the sand, until the water ran round her slim ankles.

"It's heaven," she said.

He grinned at her, raising himself on one elbow.

She began splashing her bare arms. She looked up suddenly, appealingly, and as if on some daredevil impulse. "Darling," she said, "let's take a dip."

His grin broadened. "Sounds okay, only I don't happen to have a swimsuit."

"Neither have I. What difference does it make?" She began slipping out of her blouse.

He sat up, unbelievingly.

"Say, you really mean that, hon, don't you?"

"Not a soul can see us," she said.

She stood a yard from him. The evening light glowed around her turning her slim figure to curves of gold. He would have done anything to please her. The moment, the place, the girl suddenly caught him in a spell which swept everything else from his mind. He wasn't his own boss anymore. Just for a moment he'd forgotten the inn and why he was there. He stood up, peeling off his jacket.

"Say, why not?" he said, and threw his jacket to the ground. "If you want to play, kiddo, so will I."

She saw the holster under his left armpit as he took his draped jacket off. She stared at it, a fixed smile on her mouth, until his little laugh dragged her eyes to his face, and the look on it as he came towards her.

Chapter Twenty-Two

P.C. FRANCIS PUT down the telephone and scowled at the notebook on his desk. Everything always came at once and at the wrong time. After weeks without even an incident worth mentioning, he was suddenly inundated with calls, instructions and journeys, just when he needed to spend every spare moment with his sweet peas. There was no end to do before the flower-show at Thallerton a week hence. And he'd had every hope of carrying off the top prizes in the classes he was entering.

He loved his garden, and when he had been transferred from the busy town of Sharbridge to Pebcreek a year before, he thought he had found the haven that would comfortably see him over the last few years to his retirement. The house had been up no more than three years and had every convenience for his wife, the garden was large and already well cultivated, and Pebcreek was a quiet backwater.

The job was smooth, routine. More paper work than at headquarters, of course; farmers' livestock movement records to sign, cattle and pig movement licences to issue, and reports for H.Q.; such items were straightforward enough once he was used to them, and if the area of his rural beat was a world of difference from his town patrol, it was pleasant country. He didn't dislike the cycling that made up much of his working hours. Even the night duty, when on occasion he had to rendezvous with the sergeant from Thallerton and his own opposite number from Cannel at their conference point, was better than patrolling about the town, trying the doors of shops and other business premises to see that they were secure, apprehending a drunk, or reporting a traffic offence.

He read the details he'd just recorded in his notebook again. Obviously headquarters thought the find important. The super at Sharbridge had been on the phone himself. Had only just given him all the details. He'd treated the matter urgently.

With a deep sigh P.C. Francis got up from his desk, glanced round the little office for his helmet, and grabbed it from the peg behind the corner. He'd have the super and the sergeant and various other official bods on his heels over this, that was for a cert. After months of plain routine it had to happen now, just when the show was coming. And to make things worse the damned greenfly earlier that evening were getting at the sweet-peas.

His inspection of the vestry and the underground hiding-place for the sacking-covered chunk of machinery hadn't got him very far. Not that he thought it would. The discreet inquiries which he had subsequently made among the one or two likely sources of information in Pebcreek hadn't got him much further either. He had come back, unmoved by failure, knowing that his colleagues in the other areas of the division would get the same reaction.

There was no time to sit down to tea with his wife, let alone to see how the sweet-peas were making out. He drank a cup of tea in the kitchen, swallowed a piece of cake and went off again on his bicycle. It had been a hot day. Now a light breeze was blowing up-river from the east cooling the heat of the afternoon sun. P.C. Francis liked the river road, even in winter. He liked to hear the wildfowl calling to each other across the marsh. Often he'd stopped to admire a flock of mallard silhouetted against the cold evening sky, winging their way towards the coast.

But his mind wasn't occupied with such things now as he dismounted and began pushing his cycle up the incline past the ruined church. He was thinking that the superintendent had acted quickly enough. Within a few minutes of his own arrival at the church earlier, a police-car and van had arrived and the super, a sergeant and a detective-constable had made a thorough examination of the place. Eventually everything had been loaded into the van and they had all returned to Sharbridge. He had been sent back to Dormouse Creek to carry on with routine inquiries which might yield some hint of the identity of whoever it was who'd stuck that darned lot of machinery there.

He paused now in the shade of the trees fringing the old graveyard to mop the perspiration from his brow. He couldn't see what all the fuss was about, even if a blessed printing-press had been found there. But it seemed that the gaunt, unsmiling individual who'd driven up in a mustard-yellow car while the super had been there and had gone into a brief conference with his nibs, attached quite a bit of importance to it. The famous criminologist, Dr. Morelle, he was down from London. He'd heard the sergeant tell the detective-constable that he was visiting the *Moya*.

He knew the owner of the *Moya*. The bird-watching woman. Bit eccentric; it occurred to him that a lonely houseboat on the mud in a creek was a queer sort of haunt for the sort of big shot this Dr. Morelle was supposed to be. Then there was somebody else on their way down from London, too, probably to-morrow. A friend of Dr. Morelle's from Scotland Yard.

P.C. Francis brushed a gnat off his nose. Of course it was Dr. Morelle's secretary who had found the secret of the vault, he remembered. She was staying on the *Moya*. That explained, he supposed, why her boss had shown up, and it was his secretary who'd seen the mysterious someone in the church ruins. She had seen a limping man while she'd been sheltering from a storm. She had tipped off Dr. Morelle with the result that there was this commotion. The Scotland Yard inspector was coming down to take a look at things, unofficially. Headquarters hadn't called in the Yard yet. The super was handling the case. But the Scotland Yard bloke must have some good reason for poking his city-slicker's nose in.

P.C. Francis pushed his helmet further back on his head. Limping man? He'd never seen any man with a limp on his beat. What could the young woman have been talking about? Imagining it all, he reckoned. He knew everyone around these parts, and there just wasn't a man with a limp. There was an old boy with a crooked shoulder who lived the other side of Pebcreek, some chap who'd come from over Ipswich way, who'd bought a farm-worker's cottage; and there was Mrs. Dice in the village with her poor club foot. He took off his helmet and wiped the inside of it with his handkerchief.

He glanced around the churchyard and shook his head before pushing his helmet back on it. There was nothing he could do here. He had entertained the idea that he might nose around and pick up a clue. But the lot from Sharbridge must have given it all a thorough going-over. He had about as much chance of finding anything they'd missed as he had of meeting this limping man. He was about to turn and get on to his bike when there was a sudden movement behind him that brought his head round. Suddenly, although it was warm, he felt a chill in the air. He gave a little shiver and wheeled his bicycle along the path towards the vestry. He could see the door, closed now. But there was nothing else. Then there was the movement again, a scuffling in the weed-infested hedge beside him, and then a bird flew out squawking in alarm. Must have been a fox or a stoat disturbed it, he decided, and swallowed, relaxed again.

With a sheepish smile to himself, he turned the bicycle back along the rough path, pushed the machine to the crest of the rise, and mounted. He was able to free-wheel practically right back into Dormouse Creek. He was thinking about his sweet-peas.

He rode up to the village store, just in case old Greer had thought of anyone since he'd called there earlier in the day. Friendly, helpful type, old Greer. He'd had the little business for years and knew everyone and everything that went on around him. If there had been a limping man in the vicinity, he would have known about it. He saw him through the back of the shop in the store-shed, his wife was serving. P.C. Francis chatted with her, until her husband appeared, stroking the faint stubble on his chin, his fingers making a rasping sound.

"Can't say I've any new ideas," he said. "No strangers around that I can recall who walked proper, let alone one with a limp."

P.C. Francis chatted for a bit more, mostly about the flower-show and his prospects, and then got on his bicycle and rode away homewards. The large nickel watch on his sunburned wrist said seven twenty-five. But it was a bit slow. Passing The Wildfowler he eased his speed, wondering if he should look in there again, in case the limping man had appeared in the bar, asking for a pint. P.C. Francis grinned to himself at his little fancy. He remembered the sense of urgency in the super's tone over the wire from Sharbridge and all the notes he'd jotted down.

The super didn't seem to understand that if there was a stranger in the neighbourhood, especially someone with such a distinguishing feature as a limp, the whole of Pebcreek would know about it. Talk about the underworld's grapevine, it was nothing to the speed and the wide range of village gossip.

Still, he put his foot down to balance himself while he deliberated, should he call in just to make sure the man at the Wildfowler hadn't misremembered something which might prove a bit of a lead. The Wildfowler chap wasn't a real local, after all, some ex-army type or something, who'd bought the little pub with his gratuity. So he wasn't likely to know when a stranger was around.

He thought of his sweet-peas. And as if to clinch it for him he caught sight from the corner of his eye, a tall, purposeful figure approaching the pub. He turned to make sure who it was. Yes, it was him all right, he'd only glimpsed him for a few moments as he'd got out of his rakish-looking yellow car earlier that day, but he was the once-seen-never-forgotten sort and no mistake.

Ernest Dudley

P.C. Francis watched Dr. Morelle pause briefly on the threshold of the Wildfowler, and then go in. P.C. Francis decided that the great man from Harley Street hadn't called there just for a drink, and fully persuaded that he could safely leave any little matter of eliciting further information that might be available from that quarter to Dr. Morelle, he pushed off on his bicycle, his thoughts fixed firmly now on his sweet-peas.

Chapter Twenty-Three

"IT HAS HARDLY been much of a holiday, you must admit, Dr. Morelle," Miss Frayle had said, as the Duesenberg purred along the lonely road back to Pebcreek. Dr. Morelle had smiled down at her bleakly, but offered no comment. She guessed that his mind was occupied with the outcome of the meeting that had not long come to an end at the Sharbridge police-station. She had thought she had better offer to accompany Dr. Morelle when he had informed her on their return to the *Moya* following the discovery under the old church. He must acquaint the local police, as well as Inspector Hood at Scotland Yard, of this new development which he suspected was linked with the presence of Johnny Destiny in the vicinity, Miss Frayle's account of the limping man and a certain individual named Danny Boy.

Rather to her surprise he had accepted her offer to go along with him, she had fully expected him to reply that he could manage to confer with the local police without the stimulation of her presence, or words to that effect. But, no. "There may be a few notes which I should be obliged if you would make, Miss Frayle," he had said. "If you could forego whatever excursion you were planning with your friends for this evening."

In fact, Erica Travers had complained that she felt a bit of a cold coming on. She must have got chilled as a result of the swimming-party at the Dormouse that morning. "You'd better stay out of the breeze," Aunt Edith had said to Erica. "Make an early night of it, you don't want it to develop into a bad cold."

And so after tea Erica had pushed off to bed. "Not to worry about her," Aunt Edith had said to Miss Frayle. "You pop along with the Doc, I'll look after Erica." Miss Frayle had smiled at the expression on Dr. Morelle's saturnine features as he caught this abbreviated reference to himself.

And so, leaving Aunt Edith to fuss over Erica, Miss Frayle had accordingly set off with Dr. Morelle for Sharbridge. She had no inkling in her mind of what lay behind Dr. Morelle's ready acceptance of her offer to accompany him. It had not occurred to her that he felt less uneasy knowing that she was under his watchful eye, while Erica was also safely aboard the houseboat, against the possibility that Johnny Destiny might learn of their presence in the vicinity and take appropriate measures to deal with two people whom he would consider a distinct threat to his freedom.

In fact, there had been no need for Miss Frayle's assistance when she and Dr. Morelle had arrived at Sharbridge. She had waited about outside the superintendent's office, while Dr. Morelle talked to the superintendent himself and two or three other police-officers who popped in and out. She knew that Dr. Morelle had spoken on the telephone to Inspector Hood at Scotland Yard, and she had asked him to give her love to the other. Afterwards when she and Dr. Morelle were in the car, heading back to the *Moya*, he had mentioned that he had conveyed her greetings to Inspector Hood and that he would be coming down from London next morning.

It had been stuffy at the police-station and she had been glad when at last she was in the Duesenberg once more, Dr. Morelle silent and brooding beside her. Idly she watched the changing pattern of the scene go past: meadowland and cultivated fields, marshy pastures and reed-fringed dykes; the shady pools and tidal creeks, everywhere there was so much space in which to breathe. The great expanse of sky ahead that heralded the approach of the sea, the rich blue sky with darker hues low down across the eastern horizon, tinged with pinks and mauves and just above them, faint reflections thrown up by the sinking sun.

A light breeze blew across her face full of the scent of sea and marsh. But it did not sweep away the enigmatic expression Dr. Morelle wore.

A couple of miles the Sharbridge side of Pebcreek they met a police-car. The patrolmen saluted as it went by and Miss Frayle was intrigued that Dr. Morelle should be recognized in the brief moment of passing. Though, of course, they would recognize the car. "It looks as if we've started things moving round here," she said. He gave her a silent nod. She observed the breeze whip at the greying hair of his temples beneath the pulled-down brim of his dark hat. There was a little colour in his usually ivory features, and she thought he might have been caught by the sun.

There was little traffic on the road, and Pebcreek village presented the same sleepy appearance she had come to know. They drove through it slowly. There were few people about. Some children on the green, and an evening fisherman putting off in his boat. Was it only the day before yesterday when she had arrived and viewed the rainswept scene with sinking heart? Was it such a little while back since she had stumbled about the old graveyard, full of twilight shadows and fears? It seemed as if she had been there for weeks, so much had happened. And as she had said, it hadn't been much of a holiday, so far. All the same, she had to admit, with a glance up at Dr. Morelle, she was enjoying it.

The powerful engine of the 1934 model SJ, super-charged Riviera phaeton took the gradient without the slightest change in its throbbing rhythmic note, it crested the top, and down the other side.

The discovery under the old church might appear a somewhat unlikely set-up for a big-time operation planned by the last remnants of the Transatlantic gang, Dr. Morelle was thinking, but because it was unlikely it had from the counterfeiters' viewpoint that much in its favour. Such a place as the old church might well appeal to Johnny Destiny, if he had run his ex-confederate to earth in this isolated part of the world. The manner in which he had covered his tracks on the way to England, revealed that he had a good reason for coming over. Dr. Morelle felt confident that Destiny would not have been in the vicinity unless he had a strong motive.

He wondered where the artistic-minded Danny Boy could be. The counterfeiter, whose skilled fingers could achieve such convincing effects, certainly might have chosen a worse place than this part of the world in which to hide himself. It seemed to Dr. Morelle that it possessed only one disadvantage, which was that by virtue of its very isolation a stranger appearing in the neighbourhood might be expected to excite some notice and comment. On the other hand, Dr. Morelle reflected, it was all of three years since Danny Boy had last been heard of. Time enough in which to become part of even the smallest community, so that he would by now no longer be regarded as a stranger.

Arrived back on board the *Moya*, Aunt Edith showed a sudden interest when Miss Frayle mentioned that Inspector Hood of Scotland Yard would be coming down the following day. "Meaning you'll be here to meet him?" she said to Dr. Morelle. He nodded. "Meaning you'll want somewhere to stay the night?" He looked at her as if this hadn't occurred to him, and Aunt Edith went on. "Better stay here," she said.

So it was arranged. Dr. Morelle brought his suitcase from the car, and was given the third guest cabin. He expressed his thanks to Aunt Edith for her hospitality by praising the amenities that she provided on her houseboat. All pretence at his having casually called at the *Moya* on his way to visit Professor Stenberg was forgotten. But Miss Frayle decided to make no comment upon this.

All this transpired while Aunt Edith was preparing the evening meal, with Miss Frayle dividing her time between seeing that Dr. Morelle was comfortable in his cabin and lending a hand to Aunt Edith. After Miss Frayle had taken a supper-tray along to Erica, snug and warm in bed, she, Aunt Edith and Dr. Morelle sat down to grilled cutlets and salad. Inevitably Aunt Edith managed to steer the conversation to her favourite topic, ornithology; and finally announced that directly after supper she was heading down the creek hoping to see a spoonbill.

It appeared that while Dr. Morelle and Miss Frayle had been over at Sharbridge, Jim Rayner had come aboard the houseboat with the momentous news, so far as Aunt Edith was concerned, that a pair of spoonbills had been spotted by a fisherman on the mudflats at the mouth of the creek earlier that evening.

"Is Mr. Rayner going with you?" Miss Frayle said.

Aunt Edith shook her head, as she took a mouthful of tinned peach and cream. "Gone over to Southend," she said, "if ever he gets there in that rattletrap car of his. Won't be back until to-morrow. He popped in to say hello to Erica, and she told me when he'd pushed off that it's something about some poster he wants some background for. So he's staying at Southend overnight. Rush job, apparently."

"I'm sorry I missed him," Miss Frayle said. "Are you going off on your own?"

"Why, want to come with me?"

Miss Frayle hesitated and glanced at Dr. Morelle, who was lighting a cigarette, Aunt Edith had just served coffee. She wondered if Aunt Edith was going to ask him to come along as well. "I wouldn't know a spoonbill if I saw one," she said.

"Spoonbill, sub-family Plataleinae in the ciconiiform family Ibididae," Dr. Morelle said crisply, "and closely related to the ibises. The spoonbill is characterized by its curious bill, which is long and flat, and dilated at the end into the shape of a spoon. Hence its name. Its feet are adapted for wading, and the bird obtains its food, consisting chiefly of fish, frogs, molluscs, and crustaceans, from shallow water." He drew at his cigarette. "The spoonbill is found in Europe and Central and South Asia, and is a visitor to Eastern England. Formerly it bred in this part of the world as well. It is a rare bird indeed."

Miss Frayle couldn't help bursting out laughing at the sight of Aunt Edith's open-mouthed amazement as Dr. Morelle paraded his knowledge on the one subject which was closest to her heart. Miss Frayle was perfectly well aware that he had done it intentionally, simply to show off the far-reaching range of his erudition.

"Would you like to?" Aunt Edith started to ask him when she had recovered her astonishment sufficiently to speak, but he cut in promptly.

"The prospect of crouching in a boat, cramped and cold, frankly makes not the slightest appeal to me," he said. "Even in the noble cause of ornithology."

Miss Frayle thought it was rather mean of him. Aunt Edith would obviously have been terribly thrilled if he had gone along with her, and privately she thought that a little discomfort such as he had described wouldn't do him any harm. Impulsively she offered to go with Aunt Edith herself.

"Good for you," Aunt Edith said. "Wrap up warm and you will be all right. You might even enjoy it," she said with a sidelong glance directed at Dr. Morelle.

Miss Frayle saw him frown, and thought for a moment he was about to say something as if to prevent her. But if any reason had occurred to him to cause him to dissuade her against going on the trip, he changed his mind. He said nothing.

Presently, Miss Frayle was changing into a pair of slacks and a heavy sweater, in readiness for her trip with Aunt Edith. She wished Dr. Morelle was going with them, this time because she rather fancied herself in her get-up, Erica having expressed her admiration for her appearance in no uncertain terms. She had called in on the other on her way up on deck, and she moved away from Erica's dressing-table and glimpsed through the port-hole, which was shoulder high, the surface of the water. Hardly a ripple on it, blobs of flotsam and jetsam slipped past, a white mist was beginning to hang above the marsh. She experienced a faint pang as Erica expressed her pleasure at the fact that she wouldn't be left alone on board the houseboat. "Jolly nice to know," she said, "that Dr. Morelle's around in case."

Miss Frayle noticed that Erica was looking extremely pretty as she sat up in her berth, an attractive stole over her slim sunburned shoulders. She couldn't resist hoping that Dr. Morelle would find something to occupy his full attention while she and Aunt Edith were away, and that he wouldn't think it necessary to call in to see if Erica was all right, didn't require her temperature taking, or anything like that.

128

Not, of course, that Dr. Morelle would notice how attractive Erica looked. He never noticed that about any woman. Except, perhaps that lovely young countess some while ago, who'd given him that gold cigarette-case. Miss Frayle gave a little heartfelt sigh. Anyway, she decided, she was going to do her best not to let Aunt Edith spend too long spying on the blessed spoonbills.

Up on deck, Miss Frayle found that Aunt Edith had brought the dinghy alongside and she was already in it, waiting. She was obviously in her element as she looked up at Miss Frayle. She was wearing her canvas trousers belted round her ample waist, canvas shoes, and a heavy sweater. Around her neck in their case swung a pair of binoculars and on the stem thwart was her camera. An outboard motor was clamped on to the transom, but tipped forward so that the propeller was clear of the water.

Aunt Edith pulled the stern painter free of the *Moya's* rail. "Okay," she said. "Down you come. Dr. Morelle's got some binoculars for you."

Miss Frayle turned to him as he stood there with another pair of Aunt Edith's binoculars also in their case, ready to hand to her. She had a mental vision of her dropping them into the water, and as she hesitated, another image swiftly rose upon her mind. It was that of Dr. Morelle left behind and Erica downstairs, calling him to find some excuse to visit her. She decided he ought to have something to do to occupy his mind. She shook her head at the glasses.

"You keep them," she said. "It'll give you something to do." She hadn't meant to say that, it just slipped out. But still he couldn't know what was in her mind. Dr. Morelle merely shrugged and bent what she felt positive was a faintly sardonic expression upon her as she stepped over the rail and on to the accommodation ladder clamped to the side of the hull. She went down gingerly and stepped into the dinghy. Aunt Edith slipped the for'ard painter and shoved away from the *Moya* with the handle of an oar. The dinghy was caught up in the main stream of the tide and glided gently down the creek.

"Not much water alongside now," Aunt Edith said. She put the blade of her oar over the stern to straighten the dinghy on its course in the tide. "You get on the middle thwart. Don't stand up." Her tone was warning. "Now take up the other oar, we'll use them as paddles." She brought her own oar to the side as Miss Frayle obeyed.

"Aren't you going to use the outboard?"

"Scare every bird for miles with that racket? I brought it to bring us back." She suddenly smiled. "Paddling won't wear out all your strength. Tide'll do the work. Just need to keep her in the stream." She dug in her oar to correct the head of the dinghy.

The boat was quite roomy, it rode steadily, its wide beam making a good stabilizer without detracting too much from its lightness and pace.

Soon the old jetty and the *Moya* were lost from sight round the first bend in the creek, and Dr. Morelle who had been looking at them through the binoculars turned his attention to the scene about him.

They were Solaross binoculars, and Dr. Morelle handled them appreciatively. Glinting black die-cast light alloy body in the vulcanized leather-grained rubber covering, with large comfortable eyecups and an adjustable compensating eyepiece, with finger-tip centre screw focusing. The coated prisms securely retained by a lock-set feature, ensuring perfect collimation, and the 35mm coated object glasses meant maximum light gathering-power, the precision hinges accurate alignment.

It was approaching twenty minutes past seven o'clock when Dr. Morelle, after idly searching the vicinity with the glasses from the *Moya's* deck was attracted by a movement in the direction of The Wildfowler. Casually curious he brought the binoculars to bear on the two figures which had appeared from the inn. He held them steadily in the object glasses. One was a dark girl whom he did not recognize.

He knew the man beside her, however, he knew him all right.

A short while later Dr. Morelle had called out to Erica Travers that he was going ashore for a few minutes to buy some cigarettes from The Wildfowler, and he was proceeding with a leisurely air along by the side of the creek to-wards the inn. He paused a couple of times to look across the water as if something on the further side in the marsh had caught his attention. But he was pausing merely to give the impression to any watchful eye that he was bent on no serious purpose in his casual approach.

Now he was observing that the weatherboarding outside the inn was in need of paint, the hot sun and salt air had eaten into the window-sills and sashes. Even the sign wore an impoverished and neglected air. There was no bright tone of welcome anywhere and the place appeared deserted.

Dr. Morelle noticed the policeman on his bicycle. The policeman had paused and was looking at him as he opened the door and stepped into the uncomfortable saloon-bar. It was empty. There was some dirty sawdust on the boards, an oil lamp stood on the counter and had not been lighted. The evening light was fading outside and lengthened the shadows in the room. He could hear men's voices but no one came to serve him. He moved to the bar and leaning over the counter looked along the passage. The voices were louder, but he couldn't distinguish the conversation. Customers and the landlord, he presumed. He lit a Le Sphinx and waited, his eyes fastened on the open doorway. It was not a long wait. The conversation ceased and there was a movement along the passage. The man came to the door. He was short, thin, his face in shadow, but Dr. Morelle recalled the thin hair, the greyish features, the prominent forehead.

"It's a trifle dark in here," he said.

The other muttered something and struck a match, coming forward to set the lamp wick aflame. Dr. Morelle whistled casually to himself. It was half under his breath, but the man before the oil-lamp seemed to freeze. Then he thrust in the glass and held up the lamp in the grip of his spatulate fingers, throwing the rays of light across Dr. Morelle's face.

"I fear I may have troubled you unnecessarily," he said smoothly. "I wondered if you had a telephone I might use?"

The man stared at him. After an effort he found his voice. "No phone here."

An enigmatic smile flickered across Dr. Morelle's lips. He nodded lightly and turned and went out.

Chapter Twenty-Four

THERE WAS NO wind. The mist was rising around them, narrowing their horizon to a white circle that melted away upwards into the sky. Faint streaks of cloud floated lower towards the west. The strange solitude of the marsh in the hush of the oncoming night was pierced only by the gentle splash of the oars and the intermittent call of wildfowl beyond the walls of the creek.

Miss Frayle watched the ripples fold away from the dinghy until they spent themselves on the shelving mudflats on either side. As far as she could make out it was Aunt Edith's plan to get in close to the sedges that ran out over the mudspit forming the eastern point at the creek mouth. Beyond this the river stretching wide on its way to the sea, but uncovering extensive mudflats at low tide.

Here, according to Aunt Edith, was one of the feeding-grounds, and it was here that the spoonbills had been observed. As they neared their objective Miss Frayle felt a thrill of excitement, and found herself looking ahead for the point at more frequent intervals.

They left the Dormouse which the receding tide was quickly uncovering to port, and Aunt Edith steered the boat in towards the line of sedges that ran out from the bank like a miniature pier. Beyond, the river and great stretches of mud came into view, and Miss Frayle was sure she could see some birds wading at the tideline.

As they approached the sedges a bird suddenly arose, its startled call a shrill piping sound which died away as it winged over the river wall and across the marsh.

"Blast," Aunt Edith said, scowling ferociously.

"Was that a spoonbill?" Miss Frayle said.

"Redshank," Aunt Edith said with a growl. "It'll disturb all the others."

She gave another stroke with her paddle and the dinghy drifted in among the willowy sedge and tall reeds. "Hope it hasn't scared off everything on the flats. Quiet," she said, pushing with the oar, and the dinghy rustled in between the thick growth and they were almost hidden from view.

Aunt Edith came for'ard, binoculars in her hand, and raising herself, peered over the reeds focusing the glasses on the mudflat beyond. Miss Frayle was looking in the same direction and even with the naked eye could see the long, spindle legs of the waders dipping their long slender beaks into the ooze at the tideline, in search of choice morsels of food. A small flock of birds came across the river, circled and dropped down at the edge of the tide.

"What about them?" Miss Frayle said.

Aunt Edith focused her glasses.

"Look like dunlin." She considered for a moment. "Should have thought they would have left our shores by this time. They call in on their passage north. May is the month to see them."

"Any sign of the spoonbills?" Miss Frayle said.

"I'm watching," Aunt Edith moved to the thwart and quietly stood on it. "Ah." It was a taut whisper. Miss Frayle dared not speak. At last Aunt Edith stepped down and handed the glasses to Miss Frayle. "Like to take a peep? There's a pair of them on the spit just the other side."

Miss Frayle got up carefully and took the glasses.

"Stand on the thwart or you won't see," Aunt Edith said. "Sedge darn near blocks them from view. Wonder if I might try for a photo?"

Miss Frayle got up on the seat and focused the glasses on the spot indicated. Two long-legged birds walked about the mud at the edge of a little pool the tide had left. Miss Frayle recalled Dr. Morelle's description of the spoonbill. Each bird had a large, broad bill flattened out at the end to give it a spoon-like appearance. They seemed to use these as a sieve through which they sifted the tiny forms of marine life from the ooze. Miss Frayle found herself smiling in amusement as she watched their heads moving from side to side as they fed.

Aunt Edith anxious for her photograph while there was some light left, had found a spot into which she thought she could manoeuvre the boat to give her the opportunity of getting a picture. Under her guidance and with strict instructions for complete silence she and Miss Frayle began to push the dinghy from their bed in the reeds towards a little channel, no wider than a ditch, that cut in almost as far as the mudspit. Here, screened by a thin reed fringe, they would have the spoonbills in view without being seen themselves.

As the dinghy floated clear, guided by Aunt Edith's oar which stirred up the thick mud visible less than a foot below them, she indicated a bent stem of wood, like a slender branch of a tree, sticking up out of the water.

"When we get round, grab it," Aunt Edith said in a whisper. "Hold on to it and keep the boat steady while I shoot."

Miss Frayle pushed her horn-rims firmly into position on her nose and got ready to reach out. Aunt Edith used the oar again, careful not to make a splash, and the dinghy swung round gently towards the stem of wood. Miss Frayle made a grab for it and holding on to it from the bow, the tide slowly pushed the dinghy's stern round until they were nestling on the edge of the channel against the reeds. Aunt Edith threw a calculating eye at the light, muttered something to the effect that everybody should keep their fingers crossed, and picked up the camera, and knelt on the stem thwart all set to take her shot.

It was then that Miss Frayle saw it. She thought it was a bundle of clothes. It was floating, strangely still, caught up in the reeds, a few feet from the little channel.

Then some trick of the tide caused the thing to spin, so that the face showed uppermost. The eyes seemed to look straight at her.

Miss Frayle's scream startled the spoonbills and they immediately took wing; but they were forgotten in the horror and excitement as Aunt Edith quickly pushed the dinghy across the few feet of water for a closer look. It was a man, dressed in trousers and a shirt. Once more the movement of the water as the dinghy approached caused the body to twist uncannily. The face seemed to turn away as if coyly hiding from sight, and the dark, watery hole in the back of the head became visible. But before the body rolled over, Miss Frayle, gasping in horror, had time to see that it was the same man she had seen at the hoop-la stall at Southend Kursaal, and whose photo had been in the newspapers.

Johnny Destiny, or it had once been.

Chapter Twenty-Five

FOR ALONG time after the door closed on the dark, forbidding figure Danny Boy didn't move. He remained there, his body pressed against the bar, one hand sticky with sweat splayed on the counter, the other still holding the lamp. The flame flickered as the lamp trembled in his hand.

First Johnny Destiny, and now this.

His world was crumbling about his ears.

He heard the voices of his customers in the other bar, but they meant nothing to him. Even when the voices were raised noisily, demanding service, Danny Boy did not stir. His limbs as well as his brain seemed numbed. A lassitude crept over him, so that he no longer cared what happened any more. To the pub, the customers, to him. Even to Lucilla. The voices from the bar again, shouting for him to come and pull another pint. He let them shout and grumble on, until with puzzled mutterings, they went, their heavy boots scraping on the floor. The voices passed and dwindled away on the evening air. Then silence engulfed The Wildfowler.

He supposed that if it hadn't been for Johnny Destiny's arrival out of the blue, shattering the calm of his existence, he would have noticed what he now recalled to mind. A car and some visitors to that houseboat beyond the jetty. He would have paid more attention to the sight of strangers, even though it was not an unusual event this time of the year; the owners of the two or three boats in the creek often had friends down during the summer months. He'd taken no interest, except when the odd new face had come into the bar to be served.

He moved restlessly, a long shuddering sigh hissed through his tight teeth. He had to keep a grip on himself. He mustn't panic for Lucilla's sake. There still might be a way out. But there wasn't much time. He set down the lamp and twisted round at the sound of footsteps behind him. It was Lucilla returned. He began to think up something to say to her, to prepare her for the course of action he must take. And then it occurred to him that it was only her footsteps.

Where was Johnny Destiny? He had watched her go out with him, where was he now?

"Lucilla," he called, his voice sounded dry and harsh to his ears. She appeared out of the gloom in the doorway, and he put down her deathly pallor to the shadows about her. The old pub seemed a web of shadows this evening, he thought. His mind was so choked with his own apprehensions that her manner, the tremor in her voice as she spoke to him escaped his notice.

"What is it?" she said.

He moved to her and took her hands in his, they were icy cold, and he peered at her sharply. "Where is he?" he said, "I've got news for him." His mouth set in a bitter line. He seemed to weaken suddenly, to lurch forward so that she put out her hand to steady him. She moved closer to him.

"What —? What is it? Are you ill?"

"I got to be going," he said. She stared at him, her dark eyes dilated. "Something's happened, it looks like these parts aren't so healthy any more."

"You mean they —?"

"They've caught on," he said.

Her reaction took him aback. She gave a sharp cry as if a knife had twisted in her heart, so that he stared at her in perplexity. It was as if she was someone he didn't know, a stranger. He was seeing her more clearly. Something in her attitude and her voice, and he sensed she was preparing him for a fresh shock. "You mean they know?" she said, in a gasp of horrified disbelief.

"Know what?" his voice was rasping, a score of speculations, doubts and a flood of suspicion swept over him.

"About him," she said. She jerked her head back in the direction from whence she had come.

"Johnny?" His gaze narrowed. His boney forehead pushed forward at her. "Where is he?"

It was then that she completely broke down. Clinging to him desperately, she told him in terror-stricken whispers what had happened, what she had done, while incredulity filled his face. Beneath the impact of her words which welled up from within her, his brain reeled. Now the bad dream had become a nightmare so black it was unendurable. Only he must endure it, he must fight a way out of the meshes of disaster which had trapped him and the broken creature in his embrace.

Now he was trying to soothe her with inadequate phrases, while he tried to recover from the shock of the picture she had depicted for him, the picture in which she had deliberately lured Johnny Destiny on to his doom. She had got hold of the gun and put a bullet through the back of his head. This she had done for his sake, whose secret, whose guilt and sinister past she had known all the time. He tried to tell her that she had acted madly, that it was not the way out for them, that violence and death never did pay off. He found it impossible to believe that she could have done it.

They stood there for what seemed an æon in the silent inn, oblivious to everything while he questioned her, and she answered him as best she could. There was no doubt from what she said that Johnny Destiny had collected. She described graphically the sight of him stretched out in the water, a hole blown in the back of his head. He felt no pity for Johnny Destiny. All his mind was given to recovering from these double blows that had jolted the ground from beneath his feet.

"It's okay, Lucilla," he said, at length, his voice hardening with bitter determination. "We're not done for yet."

"But what can we do?"

"Get weaving," he said.

She raised her face to him, it was no longer the face of a young girl, no longer his daughter's face. It was someone else who was shaking her head hopelessly.

"The boat, that's the only chance," he said. His confidence flowed back into him. He forced himself to believe his own words. He managed with a tremendous effort to push aside the chaos that had filled his mind as a result of Lucilla's outpourings. He forced himself to believe that it hadn't happened. That the Johnny Destiny part of it was all a bad dream. He glanced at the window.

"Getting dark. Fetch the boat, bring it to the wall. The place at the end of the garden. I'll get the outboard." His eyes were bright as he looked at her. "Grab what you want, we shan't be coming back."

There was nothing she needed. Nothing was worth taking, all she wanted was to get away. She gripped her father's arm. All her affection, fear and courage was in the pressure of her hand.

"I'll fetch the boat," she said.

She went out and along the back of the inn towards the edge of the creek. There was no one about, no one had come to the inn, it was as if the last customers had warned anyone else that the landlord had gone out of his senses, and wouldn't serve a drink. The first fingers of approaching night had begun to wrap its cloak of darkness over the marsh and water. They

Dr. Morelle and Destiny

must get away before the moon swung up into the sky and revealed their flight.

She felt calmer, as if what she had done was something she could push aside while she got on with what she had to do now. The need for action, for decision and effort lifted the numbing horror from her mind. She felt no more fear now, only a cool determination. She had confidence in her father, she didn't think of failure now that he had told her what should be done. They would get away, somehow, somewhere.

She let herself quietly down the sloping grass wall of the creek to the sedge above the tideline. There was a narrow stretch of dry ground running along the base of the wall to the jetty. By keeping her head down she could gain the jetty without being seen from the road. The wooden structure and a slight curve of the bank screened her approach.

The clumsy dinghy floated a few feet out, nestling against the side of the jetty, its painter streaming in the water from the ring-bolt by the ladder. She managed to get hold of the end of the painter and pull the boat in, until she could climb in. She steadied herself in the boat and released the painter. The boat just floated. Using the oar as a pole she began pushing the dinghy down the creek. She bent as low as she could, and that way made no noise, and she kept herself hidden by the creek wall.

She went past the inn to the little spit of sedge running out from the bank below the wall. It was here her father had meant. She moved to the bow and pulled it up on to the sedge leaving only the stem in the water. She ran back up the grassy slope to the inn.

Danny had packed a canvas bag with a few things, then he went into the shed to get the petrol-can and the motor. After Lucilla had gone for the boat he had shut up the bar. He had left the lamp in the kitchen burning so as not to draw attention to the place being deserted. He'd got all the money from the till, every penny he possessed in his pockets. He came out of the shed with the petrol-can as Lucilla hurried silently back through the garden.

"The boat's ready."

He nodded. She took the petrol-can from him. He packed up the canvas bag and went back into the shed and took the out-board off the metal stand. The motor was an old, heavy model. He needed his two hands to carry it. He left the canvas bag and as he crossed the yard, Lucilla reappeared and he sent her to get it for him. She rejoined him and they went on down the garden together.

Lucilla took one last fleeting glance back. She had no regrets. The inn stood gaunt, its glimmering windows staring back at her. Suddenly, it seemed evil to her, as if some black, sinister atmosphere had crept up out of the marsh and enveloped the place. She and her father had found a kind of happiness there, but there had always been fear, too, long before this horror of the last few hours. She turned and followed her father across the patch of spiky grass, up on to the wall and down on to the sedge.

The tide had crept back so that the stem of the dinghy no longer floated clear. Danny Boy waded to the stem and clamped the motor to the transom, tilting the propeller shaft upward. Quickly he greased the rowlocks and dropped them into their slots.

"Ready?" Lucilla stood, waiting to push off.

He glanced back along the wall to the jetty and beyond. Everything looked okay. He nodded to her. She threw her weight against the bow and it slipped clear, as she jumped into the boat. She moved into the stem, Danny sat on the middle thwart and took up the oars.

"We'll row down a bit," he said. "The noise might give us away."

She was staring back anxiously, but there was no sign of anyone at The Wildfowler. Danny Boy rowed noiselessly through the shallows. His plan was to keep as close to the bank as possible, at the same time avoiding the main strength of the tide against which he was pulling. He was no boatman. But he'd picked up enough to know that the best way was to work with the tide rather than against it. Not that he had much choice this time.

He had used the boat in the creek before, but he'd never been tempted to go into the river. He'd never seen a chart of the estuary. If he had he couldn't have understood it. But he knew the lie of the land from the map. If they could get down the river almost to the coast, he knew there was an inlet through the marshes on the other side which would take them to Gullsand. They could leave the boat there, and eventually make their way overland to Byerton. They would still be too near Dormouse Creek for their health, but at least they had made a start on the journey of escape.

He gave a sigh of relief as they rounded the first bend. Rowing the dinghy even though the near slack water had taken up his strength. Now the jetty, the houseboats, the few buildings making up the tiny village were hidden from view by the curve of the river wall. He felt it safe enough to start the motor.

He allowed himself a passing mental picture of the printing-press, left behind under the old church. He wondered if he ever would have used it. He had built it up there over the years, more with the idea of keeping his hand in than anything else. He had wanted to go straight, really; and yet there had been times when the old yearning had taken possession of him. Johnny Destiny had been right about that. He gave a philosophical shrug. Well, he wouldn't be needing the press now. He gave his full concentration to the business of making a getaway.

He wasn't to know that the press was even at this moment reposing in the police-station at Sharbridge.

He shipped the oars and stowed them under the thwarts and Lucilla changed places with him. He began winding the starting cord, the dinghy drifting slowly with the tide. He was ready to give the cord a pull when Lucilla suddenly leaned over and gripped his arm.

"What is it?" He looked back in the direction they had come. He could hear it now. It was distant, but it was the unmistakable whine of an outboard motor at full throttle. Savagely he pulled the cord and the motor surged into life, drowning the sound of the other. He settled down grimly at the tiller.

He didn't say anything, nor did the girl.

Chapter Twenty-Six

DR. MORELLE'S REACTION to the news brought by a trembling, agitated Miss Frayle and a shocked Aunt Edith had been decisive. The final, if fatal, link had been forged which tied up Johnny Destiny with Danny Boy at The Wildfowler Inn, and the printing-press under the old church vestry. It seemed, now, that Nemesis herself had taken her part in the game and removed the necessity for the law having to settle accounts with Johnny Destiny.

Erica Travers, hearing Aunt Edith's voice raised in horror and sensing that something was amiss, had left the comfort of her cabin and come up on deck in time to hear the account of her aunt's and Miss Frayle's sensational find. But Dr. Morelle had not allowed any time for excited comment and speculation. Congratulating Aunt Edith on her common-sense in not making any attempt to move the body, he had instructed her to make her way as speedily as possible to acquaint the local police-officer of what had happened. He himself would make a return visit to The Wildfowler. The dark girl he had seen with Johnny Destiny through the binoculars might have returned to the inn and would possibly have something to say respecting her companion's sudden death. From the description of the girl he had given Miss Frayle and Erica it seemed pretty obvious that she was the one they had seen at the Southend Kursaal hoop-la talking to Johnny Destiny.

A faint light was showing through the window of the same bar where Dr. Morelle had a short while earlier confronted the landlord of the inn. Miss Frayle had resolutely insisted on accompanying him, while Erica was left to await Aunt Edith's return. Now, with Miss Frayle following him, Dr. Morelle went inside. The bar was empty. Dr. Morelle crossed to the counter and turned up the wick of the oil-lamp burning there. It flared in its globe, throwing grotesque shadows round the room. A dull reflection of the flame flickered across the bottles on the shelf at the back, like the winking of evil, shiftless eyes. Miss Frayle felt she was allowing her imagination to get the better of her and she glanced away and saw the wildfowl in its case on the wall. It seemed to be watching her, the small beady eyes in the dark plumage followed her. In the heavy silence the ticking of a clock assumed an unnatural sound.

She followed Dr. Morelle along a narrow boarded passage, but there was no sign of the landlord or the girl. A lamp hung from the ceiling in the kitchen, throwing rays of yellow light through the open doorway into the passage. The room was empty. The furnishings were poor but tidy. A folded tablecloth lay on the table, the whole place had an air as if the occupants had deserted it abruptly and it had not yet recovered from the shock.

The passage led to the scullery. It was full of shadow. Twilight had fallen, and a bright moon had started its night-ride. It's rays faintly pierced the gloom as Dr. Morelle crossed the brick floor to the partly open door. Miss Frayle followed close on his heels, relieved to get out of the place into the moonlight.

They stood still for a moment. Dr. Morelle stared across towards the river wall, peering into the distance.

"Do you hear anything, Miss Frayle?"

She lifted her head and listened. Through the stillness came the faint splash-splash of a boat's oars. "It's a boat," she said.

But Dr. Morelle was already striding along the back of the inn up on to the wall. Miss Frayle caught up with him as he gazed towards the river. It was only a speck in the moonlight, but it was a boat. The echo of its oars sounded faintly across the marsh.

Dr. Morelle spun round, and made his way swiftly, following the wall back past the inn, and on to the road. Breathlessly, Miss Frayle chased after him, back to the *Moya*. Erica came out of the deckhouse as they crossed the gangplank.

"They've got away," Miss Frayle said. "The inn's deserted."

Erica gasped and muttered something about Aunt Edith not having got back yet.

"You know the river well enough?" Dr. Morelle said to her.

"Well enough for what?"

"Well enough to keep us clear of mud-banks," Dr. Morelle snapped.

Erica gulped at him, but already he was urging her down below, ordering her to get on her warmest clothes. "You might be of some help," he said.

"Thanks," she snapped back at him. Then hurried from view. Dr. Morelle had moved to the rail and over, down the ladder, into the dinghy, calling to Miss Frayle to bring the petrol-can from the deck locker. Miss Frayle collected her confused sensations and went into action. Quickly she was clambering down to the dinghy alongside, holding grimly on to the half-filled can with one hand, clinging to the ladder with the other.

Dr. Morelle had the motor running as Erica appeared in slacks and muffled up to the ears. She stepped into the boat, and Miss Frayle cast off a bit too eagerly. The tightening painter nearly spun the bow round crashing into the hull of the houseboat. But Dr. Morelle acted in time and there was no mishap. They moved out into the creek a bit, but not so far that the motor had to fight against the full strength of the tide.

"Which way do you think they'll go?" Erica said to Dr. Morelle.

"Down river, towards the coast," he said. "Where else?"

"They might go straight across," Miss Frayle said. "Land on the other side."

"No chance of it." Erica shook her head emphatically. "It's marsh and creeks that way. You couldn't get far unless you took your boat along. No, they'll head down river, either to Gullsand on the north bank or Pinley on the south."

Dr. Morelle nodded his agreement and Miss Frayle glanced speculatively back at their wake uncoiling behind, with its dancing reflection of the moon. "They've got a start on us," she said. "They may have a motor, too."

Dr. Morelle was staring over the bow as they cleared the first bend in the creek, as Erica said to him: "This is a powerful motor, I'll tell you that. Three-and-a-half h.p. And a lighter boat." As she spoke they heard a motor start up.

"We should have every chance of overtaking them," Dr. Morelle said. He spoke confidently, turned and he sat sideways, able to see their course ahead. Miss Frayle sat sideways too, up near the bow, her eyes sweeping ahead to locate the dark streak of the Dormouse. It would be indicated by a buoy; she remembered Aunt Edith pointing it out to her. The water was flat, like a pond, tinged with a yellowish-silver, except where the shadow of the eastern wall hung over the edge of the creek. The noise of the motor drowned the rippling wash flooding the shelving mudbanks either side. The sound reverberated to and fro across the creek, setting to flight the nesting birds and wild duck over in the marsh. Above the throb of the engine and the splash of water came the warning cry of the marsh fowl as they fled wildly from the edges of the creek.

The Dormouse buoy came in view. Dr. Morelle set course across the creek in towards the mudspit and the reeds which held the remains of

Johnny Destiny. As the point came abeam Miss Frayle's eyes were irrevocably drawn to the shadowy patch of vegetation running out into the water. It looked a ghostly place in the moonlight. The leaning branch she had held at Aunt Edith's request looked like a giant grotesque arm pointing upwards out of the water. The thought of it sent shivers down her back.

Soon the point was dropping astern and they came round into the broad expanse of the river.

"There they are," Miss Frayle said, her voice high with excitement.

There was not a great gap between them and the small dark object which was recognizable as a boat. They could make out the two figures in it. Both appeared to be half-standing, half-leaning at one end. The boat ahead was close in to a great shelving mudbank and was making little headway. Beyond, the river stretched out to meet the thin veil of mist that obscured the sea. A long way across the water and marsh a light glimmered, a lonely habitat in a forgotten world. The dark blur of the mudflats and the vague line of the river wall on the further side exaggerated the width of the estuary.

"They're not moving very fast," Erica said. "We're much faster than they are."

"Don't look as if they're moving at all," Miss Frayle said.

"Listen for their motor." Dr. Morelle suddenly shut down the throttle to a low hum. No sound came from the boat ahead.

"They've got trouble," Erica said. "Looks as if they're trying to clear their propellor. Caught up some weed, I shouldn't wonder. Plenty of the stuff about."

Dr. Morelle had opened the throttle again and the boat surged ahead. His aquiline features were calm, his dark gaze was fixed ahead upon his objective. He could see the other boat drawing ever nearer. He could make out the two figures aboard. The boat appeared to be drifting slowly in towards the mudbank. Dr. Morelle saw that the man, Danny Boy, was struggling to right something low down on the propeller shaft. The girl was close to him, pointing towards them. Suddenly the man stood upright and using an oar pushed the boat round and into the mud. They both jumped out and immediately sank to their ankles. Slowly they began to move up the bank.

Erica gave a great cry of warning. The unexpected hysterical note in her voice made Miss Frayle jump. "Come back, come back," she shouted. She turned desperately to Dr. Morelle. "Tell them to come back. That's Devil's Flats. It's full of mudholes."

Miss Frayle gasped as she caught the panic-like urgency in Erica's voice. Dr. Morelle called out to the two stumbling figures ahead. He uttered the warning that they were heading for danger. But the two fugitives did not even look back. Their progress slowed as they fought to drag their feet clear of the mud that pulled at them. Dr. Morelle ran in towards the bank. He cut out the motor, and the stem of the dinghy glided into the ooze, the ripples from their wake breaking all around them. Miss Frayle stood up, swaying the boat as she called across the short stretch of mud to the fleeing figures.

"They'll never make it," Erica said grimly.

Even as she spoke there came a piercing scream from the girl and she began to sink before their eyes. Dr. Morelle was already pulling up the boards at the bottom of the boat, and throwing them out on to the mud. But they formed up a path of only a few feet. Dr. Morelle stepped out, an oar in his hand. He hurled it like a javelin in the direction of the struggling figures, but it fell unnoticed by either of them.

Miss Frayle stood in the bow, her eyes fixed on the scene in fascinated horror, as Danny Boy turned to help the girl.

He had floundered back to her, his arms reaching out to her shoulders. The slimy gurgling sounded horrible. Dr. Morelle was lying flat on the mud pushing the duckboards in front of him with the dinghy's painter running through his hands.

But the ooze worked quickly. Suddenly the girl had disappeared, silently and awfully, and only the man's head showed above the slime. Then, with a choking noise that froze Miss Frayle's blood he threw up his arms and was gone beneath the surface. The great space gurgled and filled, the glistening ooze rising up in bubbles, and where the two figures had been was nothing but whorls and snaking rings on the surface of the mud.

Miss Frayle and Erica Travers leaned over the boat to help in Dr. Morelle. Erica stood staring across the mud, while Miss Frayle sank down on the thwart, her head in her hands. The moon pushed up between some ribbons of cloud, the mists curled along the water. No one spoke. From somewhere across the river came the plaintive cry of a curlew.

It was a little while before Dr. Morelle started the motor.

Chapter Twenty-Seven

"AND OF COURSE," Miss Frayle was saying, "it's obvious how you guessed it was that poor man Danny Boy, when you went into the inn."

It was the following day, before lunch-time, and Dr. Morelle and Miss Frayle were in the study of 221b Harley Street, where they had arrived an hour before. Dr. Morelle had left Inspector Hood who had arrived as arranged at Dormouse Creek that morning, to tie up any loose end that had remained from the night before. Not that there appeared to be very much uncompleted business left to take care of. The deaths of Lucilla and her father provided a not entirely unsatisfactory solution to the problem of dealing with Johnny Destiny's killer, while at the same time there was little need to probe any more deeply into the mystery of the limping man and the printing-press under the ruined church. It was obvious that it had been Danny Boy whom Miss Frayle had seen coming out of the ivy-covered vestry that stormy evening, he had deliberately assumed a limp, realizing his presence had been spotted, in order to divert the possibility of suspicion from himself.

Inspector Hood had agreed with Dr. Morelle that the Transatlantic dossier could now be counted on as finally closed.

Dr. Morelle expelled a cloud of cigarette-smoke ceiling-wards and raised a quizzical eyebrow at Miss Frayle. "Do you know," he said, "I can hardly wait to learn how I succeeded in persuading the landlord of the Wildfowler to reveal his identity."

"Because of that tune you whistled when you saw him," she said promptly. She began to hum a strain of the Londonderry Air. "The moment he heard it, he realized the game was up."

"Brilliant, Miss Frayle," Dr. Morelle said. "And, naturally, as always you are perfectly right."

"Oh, Dr. Morelle," Miss Frayle said.

There had been nothing for her but to cut short her holiday aboard the *Moya*. Quite apart from the fact that there was a certain amount of work entailed as a result of the dramatic happenings at Dormouse Creek, she herself couldn't have stayed there an hour longer than was absolutely necessary.

To her the whole place seemed haunted by an atmosphere of horror which no sunshine the next morning could disperse. The murder of Johnny Destiny and the ghastly end of Danny Boy and Lucilla. One loose string which had so far not been tied up conclusively concerned Johnny Destiny's end, though all the evidence pointed to the girl having shot him. Dr. Morelle had witnessed her and Johnny Destiny together; and only a little while later had met Danny Boy in The Wildfowler, which seemed to indicate that the father could not have been guilty, and that it therefore followed the girl was.

What had been her motive must forever remain a matter for some speculation. Jealousy? Because she had discovered the object of his visit to her father? It could have been either of them. Dr. Morelle and Inspector Hood had postulated both theories, but it could have been something else again. Anyway, it was profitless to conjecture, possibly some fresh evidence would arise before the case was finally closed which might give the answer.

Dr. Morelle resumed dictating some notes to Miss Frayle when the telephone rang jarringly so that Miss Frayle gave a start. Dr. Morelle threw her a faintly mocking look. "I fear your nerves really are on edge, my dear Miss Frayle," he said. "Obviously you very much need the holiday which has been so unfortunately interrupted."

"I know," she said quickly, as she crossed to the telephone. "Perhaps I can make a new start in a day or two, when this lot is finally cleared up, and there won't be anything else to worry you."

The corners of his mouth twitched with the barest flicker of chilly humour at the implication in her tone. She really did believe that she was indispensable to him, that without her at his beck and call the world would stop spinning for him. He scowled slightly to himself, his dark brows drew together as he recalled what it had been like in the past when she hadn't been on hand.

She smiled at him sweetly as she lifted the receiver. "This'll be Inspector Hood," she said, "with some more news for you from Dormouse Creek."

But it wasn't Detective Inspector Hood's warm and familiar tones which came over the wire. "It's Mr. Beaumont — tell Dr. Morelle —"

The voice exploded in her ear in near-hysterical agitation. She turned to Dr. Morelle, her eyes widening behind her horn-rimmed glasses. He gave her a quizzical look across his desk.

"It's Mr. Beaumont," she said to him.

He tapped the ash off his Le Sphinx and crossed to her, and as she was about to hand him the telephone the voice from the other end rattled her eardrum once more. "It's my father — I've just found him dead — in his bath —"

Miss Frayle rolled her eyes expressively upwards, as Dr. Morelle began speaking incisively into the phone. It looked as if any hope she might have had of picking up the thread of her broken holiday was rapidly receding for this summer.

If you enjoyed *Dr. Morelle and Destiny*, please share your thoughts on Amazon by leaving a review.

For more free and discounted eBooks every week, sign up to our newsletter.

Follow us on Twitter, Facebook and Instagram.